FIRE IN MIND

BY

JULIAN M. MILES

Published by Lizards of the Host Publishing

First edition (published privately) November 2011

Second edition published by Lizards of the Host Publishing April 2013

This paperback ISBN: 978-0-9576200-0-1

Ebook (Smashwords Edition, multi-format) ISBN: 978-1-4658-5936-5

Cover design and layout by Julian M. Miles

Original front cover art by Carl Critchlow

Printed and bound in the UK by Inky Little Fingers

Visit us online

Julian M. Miles (a.k.a. Jae): www.lizardsofthehost.co.uk

Lizards of the Host Publishing: www.lizardsofthehost.co.uk

Inky Little Fingers: www.inkylittlefingers.co.uk

Carl Critchlow: www.carlcritchlow.com

This book is humbly dedicated those who laughed, cried, applauded and otherwise enjoyed my storytelling.

Without your encouragement of that,
I would never have started this.

Contents

INTRODUCTION:
A TIME FOR FABLES

Between the fall of the age of magic and the rise of the age of reason

there was another time, an age lost to history, where great empires

flourished and wonders did not need to hide themselves from man.

History itself is not as ordinary as we are told. Magic is a part of this

world. Denial does not prevent it touching our lives in so many ways.

There should be more time for fables in this world. The wonder of having your own or your loved ones' imaginations inspired, or the empathy struck between strangers upon mutually appreciating a tale told at a gathering is something we should all know, at least once. That moment when the storyteller's voice fades and you see what is described as if you are there.

There is a magic to be found around a storyteller's fire. One day I hope to meet you at a gathering so you can experience it for yourself, or to share a moment as you renew your acquaintance with the sense of wonder so important to us all and so often lost in the concerns of today.

***

This book started out as a collation of my fireside, gathering and Eisteddfod tales. Carl's art for the cover inspired another story, as did the title when I decided upon it. To achieve my goal of having around two hundred pages of fiction, I added two tales from my archives that felt right.

***

For those who have heard my storytelling, the stories you read in this book will differ from the tales you have heard. The printed page gives scope that a telling does not permit, as each audience has the story tailored for them, for the setting where the telling occurs and the time available. I hope you enjoy the definitive versions as much as you did the spoken originals.

***

If you are only just discovering my work, I wish you enjoyment and wonder with every tale.

THE DRAGON OF THE NESS

*A tale from the past of 'These Pagan Isles' - a Britain
not quite as mundane as history would have us believe.*

*One of my oldest stories; this is the one I tell when
meeting an audience new to bardic storytelling.*

He had lived for ages; reckoned ancient even by his kind, his lair was filled with the accumulated treasure of his days. Recently he had found less pleasure in life than he had done. Days spent soaring under his Mother's rays, stooping to shatter clouds in his wake just did not fulfil the yearning in his soul. Thus his attention turned to this new race, man, who were spreading across the lands below as they made their way to greatness or destruction. Whatever their fate, they went about it with such élan, such fire. So he joined them, flying down from the northern mountains and taking mortal form as only the great drakes can do.

In the form of a wandering noble he journeyed among them, finding their strivings a tonic for his ennui, and being constantly surprised by their ability to create things of incredible beauty. But it was in a little village close to the foothills below the peaks that concealed his lair that he found her. She worked as a barmaid in the tavern, and her beauty near stopped his great heart. He was entranced. She possessed a natural grace that put deer to shame, and a laugh that brought faeries from all over to her side, not that she could see them.

He spent more and more time at the tavern, and knowing looks were exchanged between the regulars as the noble Uther visited again. One summer night he walked her home to her father's watermill, and departed with her name at last. Aeriel.

Aeriel's father was protective of his only child, but his fears were allayed by the visiting Lord's worldliness and honesty. The man was so obviously smitten with Aeriel that he couldn't even see it himself. But it near broke his heart to see his daughter cry every time that Uther took his leave. So he waited a little way down the path one night, and demanded that Uther do right by his daughter. Either make a commitment, or leave his daughter to get on with her life. It was not fair, with her refusing to even consider other suitors while Uther kept returning. Uther, as he had come to think of himself, was lost. His secret was his undoing. Unless...

He flew far into the icy north to the havens of the elder kin and spent many days upon the highest peak of the land, listening to the winds. Finally, he had guidance. Leaping high into the skies, so high that the blue faded to black, he sped across half the world to a distant land. In that place he terrorised the natives until one gave him the answer he needed. At last he settled upon a broad ledge high in a vast mountain range, just as the sun was setting. Gathering his might for what he was about to do, he put forth his power as a word: "DANU!"

The name thundered, echoing far beyond the cavern on the ledge. As the echoes died, she came. Wrapped in scarves of silken night, raven hair shining, she smiled a knowing smile as her fiery green eyes beheld her summoner.

"I am come, dragon known as Uther. What would you of me?"

"A gift, fey lady. A gift to bring me happiness."

"Mighty it must be, for I see you are beset by a malaise normally foreign to your kind."

"I am? What is this illness I suffer?"

"Love for a woman, oh dragon. A pretty problem. So, state this gift."

"I would be human. My shaping of mortal guise only lasts a moon. I would that it be permanent."

"She must be special indeed. It is done. Fly you back and when you take your manform, it will remain."

She smiled as she said it, a smile that spoke of many things. But the dragon leapt away unseeing, to fly at an incredible pace back to Aeriel.

So the noble Uther returned to Aeriel, but this time to stay. He brought gifts for the entire village and his coffer for the handfasting nearly gave

Aeriel's father a heart attack. But handfasted they were, by a druid who had to excuse himself part way through the preparation for the ceremony as his othersight let him see Uther in his true form.

The years that followed were a time of joy and prosperity, as Uther demonstrated a knack for practical work, coupled with a strength and endurance that the village gossips were sure kept the spring in Aeriel's step. But the couple remained childless, a cause of great regret for all.

Eventually the servants of the lonely god came north, and a priest arrived in the village. He was a deeply pious man, who rigorously stamped out all signs of the devil's work within a few weeks of his arrival. Having overseen the building and furnishing of his church, things became a little too quiet and the priest found himself listening to the talk amongst his congregation. Of many irrelevant things to be sure, but a particular item caught his ear. The mysterious and unaging Uther, husband by heathen marriage to the lovely Aeriel. Her father and he were partners in the very profitable watermill. Oh yes, here was something that bore investigation. With proven deviltry, the watermill would become church property. The priest gave thanks to his god and set to planning.

The priest's meddling started out gently, easily dismissed by Uther and Aeriel while his rumour-mongering reaped greater harvest. Aeriel's trips to market became marked by sly glances and whispered conversations that stopped when she came near. When the local clan lord became involved, things began to turn sour. Uther could not divulge even the little lie of part faerie blood to explain his still youthful good looks. Superstition ran wild, and fear began to build, ably fuelled and guided by the priest.

Early one spring morning, about a year after the priest arrived, Uther bid a tender farewell to Aeriel. He told her that he had to briefly visit his homeland to ensure his estate had been disposed of fairly as he had heard rumours to the contrary. Desolate but resolute, he set off with no intention of returning. To save her from stoning, her father from penury, and both from eviction, the mysterious Lord Uther had to disappear for good.

Two moons after his departure, a courier in mourning black delivered the sad news of Uther's demise when the merchant ship he had taken passage upon had foundered with the loss of all aboard.

Aeriel never got over the death of her nobleman and never fit again into village life. She died in the autumn, his name her last word. Uther watched from within the forest as she was laid to rest in the churchyard, cold stone at her head, cold words from a man who never knew her at her feet. That night the priest died, curled in a foetal position on the floor by his bed with a look of abject terror frozen on his face. Aeriel's grave in the churchyard was untended, but the earthen mound on a small isle in the loch was forever garlanded with flowers. Aeriel's father never visited the church again, but did acquire himself a boat.

Uther wandered for several years, but the death of Aeriel had jaded his fascination with man and his works. One stormy night, he returned to the shore of the loch after sitting by her mound for hours. Walking to a desolate part of the shore he sat, drank the last of his water and prepared himself. With his current form, what he was about to attempt could only be tried once. He gathered what little of his power remained, taking without reserve. Then he uttered the summoning word again, in a voice that tore his throat and put ripples upon the water: "DANU!"

The shout died, then the echoes. On the shore he stirred, weakened as he had never known before. He looked about at the unchanged scene. When he looked back she was standing on the shore, that knowing smile playing on her lips.

"Greetings, Uther who used to be a dragon."

Uther straightened himself and stared down that unearthly gaze.

"Greetings, lady. I did not enquire well enough about the limitations of the gift you granted. I would have it revoked."

"Revoked? You would have me take back my boon?"

"It is no longer a boon. Give me back my form."

She paused, thoughtful. Then she smiled and there was something predatory about her mien: "I can take back the gift, but it has a price. Your wings."

A dread silence fell.

"My wings. These gifts fall a little short, do they not? Mortal form but not mortal span, dragon form but without wings. I see a balance, but it is harsh."

"Unseelie power, unseelie gift, unseelie price: Unseelie balance."

Uther looked about, then down at the waters of the loch. He smiled.

"I accept. Give me my form back, without wings. I shall find a way to fly."

She laughed, clapped her hands and vanished. Uther shimmered and the nobleman fell away. Something powerful leapt into the loch with a cry of relief.

*

It is said that something inhabits Loch Ness, and on moonlit nights you can hear it crying. But for those touched by magic, it is not a wordless cry. It is a gentle sigh:

"Aeriel, Aeriel."

***

THE SORCERESS AND THE DANCER

A tale from the realm of Khyr, drawn from
the earliest folklore of that mythical land.

9

She lived in beauty, a child of nature so closely bound that her parents delighted and despaired. She could bring birds from the trees to her hand with a gesture, but other children found her strange and too true to bear. So time passed, and she grew to a womanhood of rare beauty, a slip of a thing in gowns of autumn hues, forever wandering the woodlands around her parent's tower.

On one of those wanderings she strayed across the stream into the forest primeval, entranced and disturbed by the longing she felt. As she walked, forest life flowed about her, glorying in her presence. Then she heard a noise drifting on the breeze, a simple melody unlike any birdsong or sidhe reel she had heard before. Curious, she stepped lightly, following the sound.

Revelan was a gypsy boy, dark of looks and lean of build. His hair fell like darkness that flowed about his shoulders and his eyes were blue like ice bordered pools under a winter sky. But any who thought him cool were disabused of the notion when they saw him dance. Brother to musicians and son of the road, his dance brought the journey to the audience, the slow trudge of the rain-swept heath, the bright step of a summer glade.

Within that sun-dappled glen he beheld a sprite and she saw an elemental. Both froze entranced while far away her father looked up as three deep strikes echoed through his study. A fate had been bound.

Revelan smiled and stepped lightly again, a quick eastern jig in a coastal style. She laughed and clapped her hands, and the trees took life as all manner of small creatures erupted away from the sudden sound.

She paused at the edge of the clearing, and he extended a hand to this vision, sure it would fade as the mirage it so obviously had to be. But his dream placed her hand in his, and they spun through an afternoon of laughter and dance instruction, then as evening stole over them, settled to conversation and more laughter.

Night fell and he bade her dwell, but she demurred, saying her parents would worry. So she left and he felt the night a little colder for her leaving.

She sped home on feet seemingly of light, not a branch daring to interrupt the song of her soul as it spun within to the unheard rhythm of a gypsy drum. It was in this never before seen mood she arrived in her parents presence, brought to instant stillness by their conjoined gaze. From her mother she felt disappointment and deep, deep sorrow. From her father she felt disappointment and brooding anger.

"Step ye with commoners, oh daughter mine?" he queried in an icy tone.

Her mother laid hand upon his arm, "Nay, she is young in these ways, and it was only a matter of time."

Confused, she looked from one parent gone strange to the other.

"What have I done?" she cried.

"You said always to follow my feelings. Revelan offered to teach me to dance, and my soul cried 'yes' like a bush cries for rain after drought. How can my following my heart offend thee?"

Her mother looked down and then away as her father grew stern with a sigh: "Daughter mine, you know how it goes. You are a sorceress, child of witch and wizard. The man you take to your bed and your heart will be a wizard, or better a sorcerer. Not some vagabond who dances through the woods as he no doubt does life itself."

"No!"

She strove to keep her voice calm as tears started down her face: "He is good for me, I felt it. Should your daughter not follow the instincts you bequeathed her? Should I not follow my heart if my head feels it true? What have I done that is so far from you?"

Her mother turned, resolute in sorrow: "Oh, my child, he is a memory to smile over years from now, but beyond that, your blood is too much for mortal life to contain."

She lifted her chin, her confusion crystallising to anger in the flick of a faerie wing: "He said he would await me tomorrow, and we could dance and talk again. So I will!"

But on the following morn, she found the clearing bare except for a small cairn of white stones and a gypsy rune of lament. For her father knew the ways of youth, and knew a dose of torpor dust to be the gentlest way to ease a mortal soul away from the body, never to return. He was silent as he heard her leave and quieter still upon her return, as her mother eased her distraught spirit with love undying and charms of subtle hue.

But ever after she took to wandering far afield, until the day came when she returned late upon a Hallows night, hair wild and eyes aflame. Her father knew the sign of the wyld and in a moment decided that a simple step was all that was needed to protect his misguided child. He raised his hands to her as he had never done before and wove a binding out of misguided love:

"By my life in blood-given power to you
As you love your mother this work be true.
I gave you fire, and air, and rain.
But upon this earth you shall not dance again.
Save you do, then by blood to your life given,
Your soul be forfeit and your wheel be riven."

She fell down fatestruck and heartbroken, and on recovery her silent wanderings took her further away, until one day she did not return. Her mother cried for days, yet her father cried only for an evening, safe in the knowledge that the fate-binding charm would ensure his daughter could come to no harm.

*

She travelled the land as a gypsy would, but never found her Revelan. In the great seaport over the mountains, she found a society of grace and favour where her arts of herb, pen and brush earned her patrons and some little fame.

Once she was settled, her time in the wood beyond the forest faded like a dream, and she described herself to her new circle of friends as a foundling raised by a kind gypsy family.

So it came to pass that suitors came to her door and offered to show her the many distractions of the city. One of them took her to the theatre and there she saw him again. She sat entranced through an epic of betrayal and soaring hope, watching her Revelan move like wind over a field of wheat for all that gravity seemed to trouble him. His hair was red now and his youth had given way to the smouldering confidence of perfect health and knowing grace.

She left her hopeful consort without a glance and waited at the stage door, unseeing of the strange looks she received from the patched rabble around her. Finally he came, all smiles and courtesy until she cried: "Revelan!"

He stopped, his smile vanishing like mice before the hawk. He turned a cold glance upon her and spoke in the tones of one deeply offended, "You do yourself a disservice, lady. None can be like him, and that we all know."

The crowd parted so the two faced each other across an anticipatory silence.

Her voice faltered as her smile faded, a whisper falling with never a hope of being caught: "You speak as if he were dead, but he was so full of life when I saw him."

He paused, a mind as agile as his movement flickering momentarily behind his eyes: "He died more than seven winters ago, lady. Far from here, up in the wildwoods they found him. Elf struck, they reckon."

His reflexes were the only thing that saved her from a hard fall as his words took the light from her mind.

She came around in a room hung with drapes of rainbow hue, each secured by a pair of daggers with handles that complemented the colour they impaled. From each dagger hung a musical instrument and all were clean with use and care rather than the studious cleanliness of the trophy.

"So she who weighs less than the sparrow and has the looks to fell kingdoms is awake?" The gentle bantering tone came from behind the divan where she lay.

"You mock me, for I know myself to be eldritch and strange." She sat up and swung about in a manner more suited to a cat than a lady in an evening gown. Her tense face relaxed in surprise as his teasing smile opened into a tavern warming laugh.

"Eldritch and strange? Oh, lady, lady. Would that all the women of the *world* were such, if that be what it is called."

She tilted her head like a bird regarding a sparkling bauble.

"Why should they all be as unappealing as me? Do you hate them that much?"

He sat, realising the devastating truth in her questions. She did not know that men whispered of her beauty from tavern to mansion. She did not care that every woman in the theatre-set dreaded the day that this doyenne of desire chose to go seriously looking for a man.

He stood and bowed, "You are not *that* unappealing" he said with sombre voice, but the smile he wore as he peered up through his unruly hair gave a lie to his words.

"But it *is* clear that you have been grievously misled. Please allow me the honour of clearing your eyes and mind."

She would never know what made her agree, taking his over-elegantly proffered hand while crying with laughter.

*

They became the toast of the city, at home singing shocking shanties in dockyard taverns, or smiling quietly through a performance of chamber music in a lord's mansion.

But when he danced, she would only watch. He had seen her humming little tunes and making a single step, always to stop with a frown. He knew she would put legends to shame if only she put steps upon a dancing floor. But she never did.

He had started the relationship with what he thought to be an advantage of years, but as time passed it became a disadvantage. His youth of dancing exuberance had placed great strains upon his frame, and although as limber as ever, he knew by the blood at inopportune times that his days were numbered.

She saw the claret stains upon his shirts, kerchiefs and sundry neckwear, but being a child of centuries rather than decades, she was entirely unknowing until a goodwife laid the dreadful secret bare in harmless tattle.

Mortified she fled him, grief and guilt and anger at her ignorance combining into a towering rage vented in a fury that broke porcelain all over his attempts at apology and protestations of sorrow in not telling her the awful truth.

Gone she stayed while anger faded to hurt and finally to a deeper love. She raced back to him, and upon a balmy summer evening she came to his door to find it open. In the hall there stood a silence, and on the stairs she found an absence. In his studio she found a little pile of white stones, and the gypsy rune for lament.

It was there that they found her, hair spread like waves washing against the white stone shore of the mourning cairn. In puzzlement they laid her to rest next to him in the crypts, saying she had died of a broken heart.

But a few gypsy elders traced the marks in the dust of the studio floor. They knew that she had danced for his passing as she never could his life. Making the sign of fate averted, they retreated and burnt the house to the ground before leaving the now ill-fated city.

In a far tower a wizard lay dead with a look of quintessential surprise upon his face, as if fate itself had appeared to remind him of the dire consequences for attempting to interfere with events it had arranged.

*

The witch burned that tower along with her husband's remains and returned to the land. In time she handfasted a gypsy man decades her junior. With him she chose to live but a normal span before passing, as she had heard the sad tale of her prodigal daughter's demise. She deemed that such magics as she held brought only sorrow and thus took their secrets to her grave.

***

MOTHER LOVE

A tale from the realm of Khyr, this one
from the far South of that mythical land.

Tarif grinned as the little dragon performed a graceful somersault to catch the fish head he threw it. Wonderful creatures, the Hemmenak. They had been around the fishing fleet for years, doing acrobatics, chasing seagulls, and above all scrounging fish. They would eat any part of a fish, with a seeming relish in crunching the bones.

He looked up, surveying the dockside. Every ship of the fleet had returned, and judging by the numbers of Hemmenak catching the sunlight as they cavorted, everyone had had a good trip. Tarif stooped quickly to stop another jewel blue form stealing the gutted fish from his work board.

"Away with ye, grinning thief!" he cajoled.

There was no malice involved, but like airborne cats any opportunity would be taken. The guilty party settled on the tiller and engaged the one eating the fish head in an ownership contest. Tarif laughed until he could take no more, then gutted a pair of fish and gave them a head each.

Later as the sun set, the beach and quay fell quiet as people stopped work and gathered to watch the Hemmenak dance in the last of the light before winging out over and under the sea toward the west. Their evening display was always accompanied by a gentle, humming song that brought calm to all who watched. Except one: Old Mephil sat and scowled, his catch undisturbed by Hemmenak as it always was. Tarif had never seen them near his ship in the decade since his family had arrived. Not one of the fishermen knew or would say why. There had to be a reason. Hemmenak would steal fish from the grey god himself if he wasn't looking. For the hundredth time, Tarif resolved to ask Mephil about it that evening in the tavern.

The tavern was boisterous that night, as the fishermen brought their partners down to celebrate the sudden fortune a good catch brought. Tomorrow, penury. But tonight they spread their wealth and partied like they thought the rich did all the time. Tarif was a little the worse for wear when someone pointed out Mephil hunched over a jack of ale, smoking a pipe and staring out of the window. Tarif's inebriated mind brought up the question and Tarif, being a typically single-minded drunk, wove his way across to Mephil's table. The oldster looked up with a look that would have stopped a sober man.

"Hey, Mephil. Why d'you never get Henem-, Henmak-; fishing dragons stealing your catch?"

Tarif was only vaguely aware of a spreading silence behind him. Mephil glanced at the now quiet throng behind Tarif.

"Grey god take you, you drunken excuse for an incompetent."

There was real anger in his eyes. Tarif stepped back, his camaraderie dented by the overwhelmingly hostile tone.

"Well, if that's the way you feel…"

His voice subsided to a drunken mumble, lost as he rejoined the suddenly over-loud crowd about the bar.

*

Next day the fleet set sail a little late, but in good spirits. Their three day haul to the fishing grounds was made in beautiful weather with fair winds. As they prepared the nets, Tarif turned the conversation to Mephil. His companion, Rufe, grinned and shook his head. He sat back and gazed across the water at Mephil's ship, on the far landward edge of the fleet.

"Sad story, really. Mephil used to have one of the big sloops. But he always was a stingy bastard, so his crew was the roughest bunch of swabs you ever saw. You get what you pay for. They had no respect for anything, least of all little flying lizards that stole your catch when your hangover stopped you moving fast enough to protect it. So they moaned, and they threw stones, and they tried to swat them. Then Mephil's son went down to the big city and came back with a crossbow. Never showed any of us, or we'd have taken it off him. Well I guess Hemmenak never saw one before. He got one first time, and suddenly, his sloop is the only one in the fleet without Hemmenak. Mephil junior was full of it. Reckoned we should all get crossbows, or better still hire his. He got a few lumps about that and eventually shut up. Then one night Mephil himself comes running into the tavern, screaming that a giant Hemmenak just sunk his boy's boat as the lad was long-lining off the point. We all reckoned he was a bit touched in the head after his son finally messed up while trying to night fish when drunk. He got a bit funny after that but eventually quietened down after the funeral. Then his son's body washes up on the beach. Freak thing, with us having dropped it out over the fishing grounds. Mephil went berserk, screaming about the big Hemmenak not wanting his son to rest. So he went down to the town and got a real priest to come up and bury his son all proper like."

Tarif retrieved the wineskin and then settled across from Rufe, all thought of nets forgotten.

"Was that it?"

Rufe's brow creased and he paused as if choosing his words carefully before replying, "No. This is where it all gets a little odd. Mephil ranted and raved for days after the priest left, then he and his crew got some more crossbows and some harpoons from the whalers up the coast and set off to get the big Hemmenak and prove to us that it existed. They were gone for a couple of weeks, then stopped back to provision before setting off again. This time they just disappeared. Months later Mephil sailed back in to the bay in the ship you see now, alone. He's never spoken of the trip and you've seen what happens to those who ask him. So we stopped asking."

Tarif sat back intrigued. He pondered for the remainder of the trip, his manner distracted. As soon as the ships returned to port, he made his way to the tavern as soon as he could. The conversation with the taverner went well, but was expensive.

That night the fisher folk gathered into the tavern again, and again celebrated a good haul. All except Tarif who, while drinking steadily, always watched the corner where Mephil sat. As the evening wore on, it became clear that Mephil had imbibed a little too much. By the end of the evening, his surly silence had broken into vicious, sarcastic comment on all and sundry who fell under his eye. Eventually, his painfully, bleakly accurate outbursts succumbed to the drink. At closing time people looked about, each loath to volunteer to take the old fool home. Tarif surprised them all by cheerfully stepping in, hoisting the recumbent form over his shoulder and striding off toward Mephil's house.

Next day the fleet sailed without Tarif's ship. Upon their return Rufe went looking for his friend. High on the point, looking out over the returning fleet, Tarif sat. He had obviously been crying. To one side a newly dug grave lay parallel to the one marked 'Stoll, son of Mephil'. This one had a laboriously etched piece of driftwood for a headstone, marked 'Mephil. Finally at peace'.

Rufe crouched down next to Tarif.

"What happened?"

Tarif turned glazed eyes to his friend.

"I know what Mephil saw, and I cannot be rid of it."

It took Rufe an hour and most of a bottle of brandy to loosen Tarif's tongue.

"Last afternoon, I did a deal with the tavern keeper. He laced Mephil's drinks last night, laced them with potato spirit. He also lightly salted his meal, just enough to help a thirst. I thought I'd been clever, so I could get his secrets and make him look petty for cursing me out the other night. So when everybody wanted someone else to take him home, I got the job. All the way to his place, I badgered him. Kept on, and on. Finally, as we entered his garden – have you seen it? Beautiful it is, with firegrass and wintervine. Who'd have thought it of such a mean spirited man? Anyway, he gave up. Told me to sit him on the bench on his porch, and then sit and listen. Told me not to say a word until he'd finished. This is what he told me."

Tarif upended the brandy bottle and drank the remains without pause. Not even pausing to wipe his lips, he launched into the telling, his voice sepulchral:

"I was so angry, that monster had killed my son. I got the boys to get crossbows and harpoons and hook nets, and we went out looking for it. We sailed for days, but only got a couple of little dragons. Then we came back, stocked up and lay offshore. When the little bastards flew out in the twilight, we sailed after 'em. Sure enough, way out there, it was waiting. Big it was, big as your boat, Tarif. It looked over the little ones, then spotted us and I swear its eyes widened before it dived. Well, we was ready for that, because those dragons is like dolphins, gotta have air. So next time it popped up, we put a harpoon in it. It didn't like that, and we was off across the seas. We ran for ages, this thing never tiring, never giving us a chance to get it again.

Then after three days, it dived. By the light of the moon, we saw it leap clean from the water, its hide running blood and seawater before it arched and went down. And down. The damn prow canted forward as it tried to drag us under. We laughed and joked as it struggled. Then something hit the stern hard, and we heard the planks go. Gods, we heard the planks snapping like twigs as more somethings hit us midships, keel and prow. She went down so fast it was uncanny. Then we was in the water. Lucky most of us had been on deck, waiting for the kill. We swam together, hanging off some debris. Then Manny went down, real fast like he'd been pulled. We laughed a bit, before Joe went under. We thought it was sharks, until we looked about. No fins, just little fishing dragons perched on the flotsam, watching, watching. Watching as something pulled us down one by one, each one screaming louder than the last. Then it got my leg, and down I went. But I didn't scream, oh no. I wasn't going to give the harpooned bastard the pleasure. But I looked, in those moonlit waters, and I saw the harpooned one floating there, dead. Around him swam lots of the little buggers, and some not so little ones. Them that was getting us was about twice mansize, but there was a lot of 'em. Then this one that got me started pulling me. Towed me away it did, out of the crowd around the sinking remains of my ship. Then we went down again. Hurt me ears, we went down so far. But just as I though I was gonna take that wet breath, I saw her. The bloody thing just dragged me down far enough to see her against the moonlight. A Hemmenak, but she was bigger than any ship. She looked at me, all calm and icy, and I took that breath, took it willingly. It hurt, and it was so cold. Felt it all go away, saw Stoll again. Then she was in my head. Not dreaming, she was there. Her words come to me every night:

You took my kith and kin, bitter man. So I took yours. Let this be an end to it. We shall bother you no more.

She knew me, she knew us. Them Hemmenak comes up here like toddlers to the playpen. We fishes for our lives, and it's a nursery for baby monsters."

Tarif looked up, his gaze haunted.

"In his house, there's a Hemmenak scale, all green-blue and jewel shine, but look at it. Our fishing dragons have scales like little coins. This one is his table. Big enough to seat eight men. I loved those little ones, but it'll never be the same. Never, never again."

With that Tarif said no more and sobbed like an abandoned child.

That was the end of it. Tarif told no one else and tended Mephil's grave every day until he packed his bags and went to town. Merchants from there say he's a weaver now. As for Rufe, he's doing well. Lives in Mephil's old place and runs Mephil's and Tarif's ships. But they only fish the coast these days.

***

LANCELOT BACKWARDS

*A tale from the today of 'These Pagan Isles' - a Britain
not quite as mundane as some would have us believe.*

The operating theatre fell silent apart from the low squeal of the heart monitor, its constant pitch echoing the single unwavering green line that traversed its screen. Consulting surgeon Michaela Daniels looked up at her team. She nodded: "Call it."

Senior nurse Stephanie Sykes lifted the watch on her blouse. "Janet Hutchins, died of multiple injuries from a RTA, oh-one fif-"

Her voice stopped as her eyes widened, gazing fixedly behind Michaela. She spun quickly, ready for the onset of a drunk or another care in the community failure. It was neither. A figure of smoke and shadows twisted in the corner of the room, then with a wet crackle became a tall, tanned man with a ragged mane of black hair, dressed in a tattered suit. The wild look in his blue eyes nearly distracted her from the softly glowing sword that hung from his hand.

Then his words rose from muttering to stridence: "Not dead. Not yet. Cannot be dead, not tonight..."

The figure lurched forward, slamming his off-hand squarely on the late Miss Hutchins' right breast as he raised the glowing blade high before shouting something incomprehensible and short. There was a flash of brightness, like a huge flashbulb sited on top of the patient had lit the room, then the swordsman staggered back as all of Janet's monitors went berserk, indicating lives desperately struggling to continue. Training took over, and the medical team reacted with seamless precision. Minutes later Janet Hutchins was definitely not dead, and the sword wielding resurrectionist was definitely nowhere to be seen.

*

In the disposals area at the back of the hospital, one of the big wheeled bins creaked slowly sideways as a dishevelled figure slumped against it,

26

seemingly oblivious to the rain that poured down with a cold vehemence unchanged for centuries.

He smiled. He should know; it seemed like he'd been out in it every time, usually collapsed in an out of the way corner and wrung to shivering exhaustion after another attempt to unload his destiny. The bin came to a halt with a muted clank as it came up against the next bin in line. He slid down the side of the bin and splashed down on the asphalt, his eyes closing. Just a moment's rest; the undisturbed oblivion that came only after he'd saved another one.

*

Michaela wrestled her cagoule on as she headed for the rear exit. Another Saturday night filled with saving people from the consequences of having fun, either their own or others. Plus of course the incident of mass hallucination in the operating theatre. They had put it down to faulty closures on a couple of the anaesthetic cylinders when the swordsman turned out to have been unseen by anyone outside the room. She looked through the corridor windows as she headed down past the kitchens and bedding stores. It was really tipping down out there. Which meant it was a fifty-fifty chance that her aging Fiesta would start or just chug unhappily at her while a random sequence of despair lights appeared across its tape- and epoxy- patched dashboard. She reached the loading bay and cursed herself for being lazy thirteen hours before and parking her car in the first vacant space she saw, now nearly a quarter-mile from where she stood. Pausing to peer up at a sky where dawn had passed unnoticed, it was obvious that a break in the rain was not about to occur anytime soon. Putting her head down and tucking her bag under her waterproofs, she headed out into it.

*

He came awake. Somewhere near. Soon. This was wrong. He wasn't ready. It had never done this. Shocked realisation came as he heard a distant discord; the sound of the dance between predators and prey. He had saved the wrong one!

*

Michaela was past the disabled parking and somewhere in the darker part of the car park where maintenance had not visited yet to fix the lights. Pacing rapidly she shivered and was contemplating a large latte with whipped cream when she walked straight into someone. She was about to apologise when an arm came over her shoulder and around her neck. It was wrapped in a sleeve so dirty that the smell made her gag through her panic.

"Give us the tabs, doc."

She tried to shake her head.

"Bad idea, doc. Either we get tabs or Jimmy is going to see what your ass is like in the wet."

There was a happy laugh by her left ear. Jimmy obviously liked that idea. Michaela went icy calm. This was it. Attack alarm in her bag under her cagoule, pepper spray in the pocket of her lab coat in the office. Sod's Law; the one time she was not ready. The assailant in the stinky jacket groped her with his free hand. She shuddered. Then her world narrowed to the thin blade in the hand of the speaker as he stepped forward.

"Guess we'd better unwrap your present, Jimmy."

The knife moved slowly toward her chest. Then she was flung sideways as Jimmy was thrown into the car on the right. Its alarm went off as Jimmy's arm released her, slamming her head into the chrome of the door trim. Her head swam as Jimmy started making a low keening sound behind her. A long-haired figure in a drenched suit stepped toward the knife wielder: "Not tonight, scum. The lady is not for sport."

"Oh really? Okay hero, your funeral."

The knife moved with shocking speed straight at the stranger. Who just stood there, his posture showing more fatigue than readiness. At the last moment and with a movement Michaela could not make out, he folded the attacking arm back so the knife buried itself to the hilt in its wielder's throat. Her saviour held the pose like some macabre embrace as her first attacker gargled and pawed at his nemesis. Suddenly, Jimmy stepped into view, one arm clutched to his side, the other travelling in a blur of speed toward her rescuer's head. Michaela uttered a wordless shout and she saw him twitch his head to one side as the hammer blow landed. As unconsciousness claimed her, she saw Jimmy and the suited figure slump in opposite directions.

She came round lying on a bed she that was more accustomed to looking down at other victims on. Doctor Chandrakhan smiled at her: "You are fine, Michaela. Some bruises and a small cut to your head that we have cleaned and sutured. We X-rayed your head and there are no complications. Do you feel up to talking to the police?"

Michaela nodded. A chat with the police would let her sort the events out in her own head. The detectives were polite, sympathetic and thorough. In just under thirty minutes, they talked her through the entire sequence in depth. As they thanked her and stood to leave, she enquired as to the others involved. Detective Harrington turned back.

"The one you identified as Jimmy bled to death from a significant injury to his side before the scene was discovered. The knifeman was dead by his own weapon as you witnessed. Your white knight is in ICU in a coma, saved by your warning, but possibly only from his body dying. Jimmy swung that hammer to kill. We are very interested in talking to him as he had no ID or possessions of any kind on his person. But we will have to wait until he wakes. If he wakes."

With that, they departed. Michaela lay back but the sounds of her workplace prevented her relaxing. Finally giving in to the inevitable, she got up and made her way to the ICU. Enquiring after her 'white knight', she was directed to the end bed. As she passed the curtain obscuring him from the rest of the ward, her gaze fell on his tanned features and the shock of recognition made her dizzy. The mystery man from the operating theatre!

Holding on to the frame of his bed to prevent herself falling, she ran her eyes over his outline under the sheet. A proportional, lean build indicating a very active life. If the musculature of his revealed shoulders was any guide to the rest of him, he was in superb shape. Apart from having part of his head stove in by a hammer, she reminded herself. Who are you? she thought.

His eyes opened, blue-grey and clear under the lights. She looked round for the nurse but he waved his finger in negation. She moved closer as his lips moved in words too quiet to travel far.

"Hello, lady. I trust you are unharmed?"

She nodded.

"I am glad. For a moment there I thought I would be too late."

Her brow furrowed: "Too late for what?"

"To rectify my mistake."

She shook her head: "I still don't understand."

He swallowed with difficulty and she took the hint, lifting the curtain and taking a glass of water and a fresh straw from the cabinet beside the patient sleeping in the next bed. After a few sips of water, he coughed quietly and winced in pain. Then he looked into her eyes and she saw tears in his.

"I have been such a fool. All these years I thought if I could only save enough innocents, I would be redeemed."

Michaela pulled up a chair and took his cool hand in hers. She could not take her eyes from his: "I'm still confused. Take me through it slowly."

He relaxed and smiled, a thing of incredible warmth and beauty.

"A long time ago, I saved a dear friend from death. He was a man I loved and had betrayed so very cruelly that I sought to make amends by using a family gift in his favour, against the dictates of my family. I drew on the sang réal in me and brought him back. I should have died in the doing but grace was granted and I continued. Then I realised that my continuance had been changed from a single span to one that I would dwell in until my crime had been expiated. In saving him against the night, I took his sins and atonements upon myself."

He looked at her and saw confusion in her eyes.

"I found that my family gift had become a compulsion. I saved any and all who came my way. I could not help myself and some great sinners avoided their just reward at my hands. So I went to my uncle and begged him for release. He wept for me and said such a thing was beyond him, as only Uriel could release me. But his brother could help me ensure that my penance aided no more sinners."

Michaela was fascinated but still unenlightened as the story unfolded in a whisper. She did not notice that the whisper was getting quieter and she was moving closer.

"So I went to Corbenic and pleaded for his aid. He had me quaff of his darkest brew and swear to follow my repentance without contest. From that day, my time became a series of savings broken by wandering the places I arrived in, until the gift called me to another place to save again. I felt a purpose in the calls, as if I served and saved the participants in a grand design, but never was anything revealed."

Michaela whispered questions: "What is your gift? Is it what I saw tonight when you saved that woman?"

He smiled again and she felt her heart fall. "That is it. I can save innocents from death at the devices of cold fate or bleak evil. But tonight I thought I had erred."

Michaela shook her head and smiled. "You didn't. Janet survived and so did her unborn child."

His breath caught and his eyes widened. "She was with child? Oh, blessed this night."

Michaela laughed. "You see? You did not fail."

His gaze intensified. "You are right in ways you have no ability to know."

She shook her head again. "There you go again with the cryptic answers."

He shifted his gaze to the glass and she held it while he sipped again. Placing it back, she looked at him: "So you redeemed yourself tonight by saving an unborn child?"

He looked at her with a thoughtful look that became one of enlightenment. "I did not. I atoned for his crime at last."

A tear ran down his cheek as his hands lifted and fell upon the sheet. He looked away and looked back. "Lady; you are sure that you are well and that your encounter has not left you with a hidden malaise that may strike you down unexpected?"

Michaela laughed. "I am fine, thanks to you. But that hammer nearly killed you."

His look went from joyous to sad, then back to a calm that seemed to travel from his face, up Michaela's fingers to her heart and mind. A warmth, a lightness. Serenity; that was the word. She savoured it and took in the moment; the white sheets, his tanned features, the muted beeps of the monitors. Then she realised that none of his monitors were beeping at all. There was nothing. She looked at him in panic and his hands tightened their grip on hers.

"I am killed. Over and over have I been slain. Every time I save an innocent I die for a moment, then my penance forces my continuance. But tonight, tonight I unknowingly saved a child and then thinking myself a fool in the doing, thought that I had been sent to save you, not the mother. With my gift exhausted for a while, I did what I had to."

Michaela shook her head to clear her blurred vision. He seemed to glow in the refraction through her tears. His grip tightened further and he pulled her close as his whisper dropped to near inaudibility.

"I saved you and took a mortal blow therein. But it is what I have needed for so long. I have used my gift and prevented my misuse of it, yet have never given anything that I could not replace. My atonement needed to be selfless and unknowing."

Michaela nodded. Her brother had said similar before Helmand had claimed him. She quoted his words: "You just do it without thinking of your own life. Everything given, all the time. Total commitment."

He smiled weakly, his eyes starting to dim. She reflexively tightened her grip on his hands, willing him to stay a while longer. In that moment of instinctive caring, she felt a presence slip light and gentle through her mind to borrow her voice.

"You were my white knight; now only chivalry remains."

His eyes opened fully, vigour fleetingly restored: "She said that upon our last meeting, when she would not kiss me. Lord have mercy, it is tonight."

The light in his eyes was fading fast. Michaela had to place her cheek against his to hear his last words.

"I am Launcelot du Lac, and I am forgiven at last. Oh Guinevere, I am coming."

***

SKY DRAKE

*A tale from the realm of Khyr. This one is from
the Western borderlands of that mythical land.*

Cherale considered that it was a beautiful day to be anywhere except stuck in the converted stables that the landowner had so grudgingly donated to be the school. Despite many cleaning rounds and the efforts of all the parents, the place was narrow, stuffy and still smelled faintly of manure. But it was colourful now the children had been allowed to draw on the walls with precious coloured chalks donated by a passing tinker. She would happily have taught in a cowshed to see the looks of wonder on the faces of her class as they realised that there was a far bigger world out there than the village elders told of.

She was in the midst of leading the class through another verse of today's farming lore when Billy ran in looking terrified and elated all at once. He'd been out to relieve himself and she noted that he was in such a hurry he hadn't even retied the twine that held his trews up. She held up her hand for silence.

"Billy. What's wrong and is it really so bad that you cannot tuck yourself in?"

There were a few quiet snickers at that, but Billy didn't seem to notice.

"There's a dragon in the old barn!"

Well, that was a new one, Cherale mused.

"Billy. What have I said about telling stories on days when it's not storytelling time?"

His face fell a little, but she had to suppress a smile at his inability to dissemble as he gathered his determination.

"Miss, I'm not storytelling. There is a dragon in the old barn!"

He finished in a shout and she could see that the class was getting restless with curiosity, whether to prove Billy a liar and ridicule him or to see a marvel, it did not matter. Harvest time farming lessons or a monster in the cavernous, spooky old barn? The potential thrill won out with ease. Cherale sighed while making a mental note to ask Billy later why he had gone so far to relieve himself.

"Class, tidy your lecterns and Samuel, go and fetch Mister Dangood."

Robert Dangood was the local smithy, the only person in the village who had been outside its environs. It was a bonus that he'd been a warrior and weaponsmith. Some fighting skill might come in handy if Billy hadn't merely been scared by a snake in the shadows.

The classroom was tidied in record time and Billy tucked himself in as the girls started to deride him. A few minutes after that Robert arrived, sword in one hand and Samuel on his shoulders. He wasn't even winded after the quarter mile run from the smithy. He looked about at the eager, expectant faces and then smiled at Cherale as he deposited Samuel on the floor by his lectern.

"Samuel says you have a dragon?"

Cherale smiled. Samuel always left out details; it was a cause of frustration to many people. But he was the fastest runner in the village, so the advantages outweighed the occasional misunderstandings.

"Actually, Mister Dangood, Billy reports a dragon in the old barn. He's very insistent, so I thought your presence could be useful."

Robert smiled and brought his sword forward in formal salute to Cherale, to the delight of the class.

"My sword is ready, milady. Shall we start this expedition?"

Cherale laughed and then caught herself. She stared sternly at the class until they quietened down. Then, in her very best impersonation of a serious adult, she issued instructions.

"Now we are going to take a look, class - but you must stay back a little way from Mister Dangood and myself. If anything happens to us or we tell you to run, you run all the way to the elders. Do you understand?"

The twenty-three beatific smiles and nodding heads did not fool her for a second, but it was the best she was going to get. Gathering herself, she gestured to Robert.

"Lead on, Mister Dangood. You know something of these things."

He chuckled.

"Sneaking up on dragons hidden in old buildings? Not one of my best skills, but I'll give it a try."

With that he jogged a little way ahead of Cherale and her crowd of children as they emerged from the stable block. He struck a fine marching pose and the whole class fell into a passable marching step behind him. Cherale smiled as she marched with her charges. Anything that kept them in line she would go along with. She was also impressed that he led them the long way round on the track, rather than Billy's route across the fields. If they had to run, the packed dirt underfoot would be a help.

After a short walk they approached the old barn. It stood where it had stood since being abandoned along with the Stricklade farm two decades before, slowly falling to weeds, rain and local people looking for bits to repair their homesteads. It sat back from the track across a field of brambles and nettles broken by patches of scrub grass and wild barley. Even the track that originally led to the farm was a tangle of growth. Cherale and Robert spent some time organising the children into pairs, emphasising hand-holding and looking out for each other. With the few preparations they could apply done, they crept toward the barn. It was a big place, eerily quiet in the afternoon sun. It seemed to have extra shadows about it, making the vicinity darker. Cherale started to regret bringing the children in case there was something unusual in the rundown building.

Robert sprinted ahead and crouched by the door, his dirty grey work trews and stained tan waistcoat combining with the soot that streaked his skin to provide a startlingly effective camouflage. He peered through a couple of gaps in the planking before waving them all forward. As they gathered, the strange silence suppressing their childish enthusiasm. He turned to them and whispered, "You must stay here until I call. All of you. Billy, where was this dragon when you saw it?"

"Over to the left... no right..."

Billy gazed at his hands in confusion. In the end, he gave up and held up his left hand, "That side, Mister Dangood."

Robert smiled. With a nod to Cherale, he set off at a crouching run to where the small door opened in the sagging great doors and with a quick . glance within, bounded into the darkness, sword ready. The silence seemed to deepen as no sound came from within the barn. Then with a startled shout, Robert flew backwards through the wall near the children, causing squeals of fright. Cherale was about to rush over to him when an enormous, pale blue scaled head emerged through the hole left by Robert. Great shining eyes of pastel green regarded Robert. The silence was absolute, the children motionless in fear. Cherale felt a scream die in her paralysed throat.

"I do apologise, warrior. You trod on my tail."

Robert's eyes opened wide in shock as twenty-four mouths fell open in awe. It spoke! The great head turned and regarded the group nearby. The gaze picked out Billy and the head nodded.

"I thought you saw me, little one. Thank you for not coming back with a mob of soldiery."

Robert used the diversion of the creature's attention to scuttle backwards out of range before leaping to his feet, sword held loosely in his hand as he was unsure of what to do next. Samuel startled everyone, his speech clear as he used his best voice.

"Hello, Mister Dragon. I'm Samuel. Billy is who saw you and that man is Mister Dangood, our blacksmith. This is Miss Lorris, our teacher."

The huge mouth curved into a gigantic smile. Then the head dipped in Samuel's direction.

"I am very pleased to make your acquaintance, young Master Samuel. I am Berlush, a drake of the Sky Realm. Would you be so good as to introduce me to your classmates?"

Cherale stood in astonishment as Samuel swelled with pride and without a trace of his usual stammer, painstakingly introduced every child present, even including details about their talents or strengths without any unkind words. The boy needs to be scared by dragons more often, she thought. Samuel finished his introductions and stood waiting. Berlush lowered his head until the point of his chin rested on the ground. He sighed in a great gust that scoured the detritus from the ground around them.

"A very fine class indeed. A credit to their tutor I am sure. Now, Miss Lorris and Mister Dangood, may I possibly request your assistance with a problem I have?"

Cherale looked at Robert. He looked back and shrugged his shoulders. She looked back at Berlush, surprised that she could be so calm.

"I really don't think that there's anything we could come up with that would be of use to a great drake such as yourself, sir."

Berlush smiled again: "Oh please, skip the honorifics. Berlush is quite adequate. As for what you could come up with, I hope you will be more than capable. Why don't you all come inside and sit down? Then you can see me properly and it will help me explain."

The children were nearly bouncing with eagerness. A hurried, whispered chat with Robert confirmed Cherale's suspicion that although he was wary, he was sure that the beast could have slain them all with ease if it had wanted to. So a few minutes of subdued confusion later, the entire class was seated raptly staring at the enormous length of dragon that draped the interior of the barn in loops and coils, its blue scales emitting a faint glow that softened the edges of the abandoned stuff inside and banished nearly all the shadows. Berlush swung its head quite clumsily onto an old cart bed, Cherale thought. It was as if the movement was an enormous effort to it. It scanned the seated folk before it before closing its eyes for a moment. It opened them and the huge smile reappeared.

"Now you can see me children, what makes me different from all the tales about dragons you have heard?"

Hands shot up. Cherale felt a twinge of envy. Such studious attentiveness from a class was a teacher's dream. Berlush paused a moment before calling each child by name to answer.

"Clarissa."

"You don't have any legs."

"Martin."

"You didn't flame us to ashes."

"Sally."

"You didn't eat Mister Dangood."

"Edward."

"You're bright blue. I thought dragons were only green and grey and black and dark colours."

"Amanda."

"You don't have wings."

"Steven."

"You look like a huge snake."

That last reply brought gasps of shock from everyone. Cherale tensed, wondering if being compared to a snake would offend a drake. She saw

Robert's knuckles turn white around the hilt of his sword. Berlush snorted and very old straw flew in a storm for a while. They were all covered in the end and some of the tension eased as everybody spent a while picking bits off each other. As the activity ceased, Berlush coughed ever so gently. A little whirlwind of dust spun briefly before his nostrils.

"Steven is right; I do look like a snake to you, because I have no limbs. Edward is nearly right because blue is not a colour favoured among dragons, it is very difficult to hide amidst rocks and trees if you're the wrong colour. Clarissa and Amanda were also right spotting parts of my limbless state. Martin and Sally were quite right by your standards, but by dragon standards my behaviour is quite correct. We usually prefer to remain unseen, only resorting to ravaging as a last resort."

Cherale raised her hand. Berlush actually raised a bony eyebrow as he turned his gaze to her.

"You don't seem to be able to move easily. Are you injured?"

Berlush snorted again and turned his gaze on the rapt class: "Indeed an exceptionally observant teacher. I would bet that none of you get away with much, do you?"

The almost synchronous nodding of twenty-three heads made Cherale blush. Berlush turned his attention back to her.

"I am not injured, but I am having a lot of difficulty moving. That is my problem."

Berlush rearranged himself and wood creaked ominously. Dust drifted from the old beams.

"I am a dragon of the high sky, a breed with the fewest numbers for reasons I really don't have time to relate. Suffice to say that we never touch the ground and the presence of metal causes us pain. I was making my way back to my home territory when I had a disagreement with a dragon from the ground, one like the ones you hear tales of. He and I duelled for a bit, but dragons of my blood are more fragile than those from the ground, and I had to retreat. I made the mistake of choosing a thunder cloud to hide in, and got struck by lightning. Even though I am big, nature is bigger and the bolt of lightning knocked me out. I fell into the field behind this barn. That was a week ago. If I don't get back into the sky in the next few days, I will die. The touch of the earth drags me down, and I cannot lift myself off the ground. You see, I have to get all of me off the ground at the same time so I can rise. That is my problem."

The children turned their gazes to Cherale. Their teacher was the cleverest person they knew. She realised that they expected her to come up with a solution. She stood up and looked about at the immense length of Berlush. Then Robert interrupted her thoughts: "You're actually much lighter than you look, aren't you?"

Berlush's eyes widened in surprise: "Two observant humans in a day. A wonder. Yes, Mister Dangood, I am more like a bird in my structure."

Robert's forehead creased: "If you were outside in the field and you made a tight coil of yourself, you'd only be about three cart lengths across?"

"Yes. And I would weight about as much as a few bales of straw."

Cherale had an idea.

"Trestles! We can use old beams from the barn to make them."

Berlush shook his head slightly: "I am afraid not. They are dead things. I would still be bound to the earth."

Robert stared off into the darkness in the far corner of the barn.

"You can't be supported by people either, can you? I remember an old herb witch saying that it was not the innocence of youth, it was the fact they were untouched by death, having not witnessed it or dealt it."

Berlush snorted again: "You are entirely correct. I sense that you have an idea."

Robert looked at Cherale.

"I do, but it's going to be interesting. First, I need all of the children to find logs and other wooden bits that are over three hand spans high. No nails, no fastenings. You need to get all of them and take them into the field out back. I'll show you how to lay them out."

He turned to Berlush: "Excuse us, we will have to work fast to get done before the school day ends."

"Go ahead, Mister Dangood. I admit to being intrigued."

Robert took Cherale's hand and the two of them led the children outside and set them on a huge scavenger hunt while he and Cherale walked to the vague centre of the field. Cherale turned to Robert, questions in her eyes.

"What have you in mind, Robert?"

He smiled enigmatically: "Watch. I'll explain if the children can find enough lumber to do this."

Over the next hour, the children returned with a huge quantity of wood, which Robert ruthlessly sorted, using bits he approved of to give them a better idea of what was needed. Then he started to arrange the pieces like the spokes of an enormous cartwheel. An hour later, he and Cherale were sweating hard but the children stood about regarding the sixteen huge rows of scrap wood arranged around the gap where Robert and Cherale stood. Robert pointed toward the barn: "Now, Samuel and Billy, go and ask Berlush if he would come out here."

Cherale lightly punched Robert in the upper arm. "Explain."

He smiled at her: "The children. Untouched by death. He winds himself into a coil on top of the logs, then the children crawl underneath to the places where I've marked. It's like lifting one of the big haywain wheels.

When the children are underneath, you'll be at the centre to lift his head, and the kids rise to all fours, then Berlush contracts himself like a snake, lifting all the slack bits, and just for a moment, he'll be supported only by the children. Hopefully that will be enough."

"It should be."

They spun to regard Berlush, his serpentine length stretching from next to them nearly back to the barn. It took Cherale a lot of explaining and persuading, but in the end she got the children to understand. As Berlush started to slowly coil himself onto the logs, moving with effort and delicacy so as not to disturb the arrangement, Cherale turned to regard Robert over the heads of the children. They were all thoroughly immersed in watching Berlush spiral his head closer to the centre of the improvised spoke pattern.

"And what will you be doing?"

Robert sadly shook his head. "I have experienced and dealt death. For this, I can only offer support and shout the moment for everyone to lift."

Cherale nodded, then turned to where Berlush was now a spiral of azure scales and radiance centred on his glowing green eyes. With a shake of her head, she led the children to the points where they would scrabble under the dragon before using one of the gaps left to make her way to the centre. It was warm under the dragon, and smelt faintly of summer rain in the high peaks of her youth.

She slid herself under the head, and apologised as she lay on her back and braced her feet under Berlush's head.

"Do not worry. I am not bothered by such niceties, but thank you."

Cherale shouted out: "Get ready children! Listen to Mister Dangood's voice! If anything odd happens, you remember to drop flat, do you understand?"

They all replied with shaky affirmatives. She shook her head at their bravery. Robert's voice sounded steady, his clipped tones betraying a slightly more interesting military career than he confessed to.

"Okay. I'm going to count to three and you all get ready. After three, I will shout lift and when I do that, you all push up as hard as you can. Then when I say down, you all should lie flat."

Robert took a deep breath, sent a prayer to gods long uncalled and started: "One. Two. Three. LIFT!"

He paused but a moment. Berlush did indeed seem to rise in places: "Berlush, now!"

The great drake tensed himself, the pulse of effort knocking a couple of children off balance, but they held. Robert waited for something startling, but after a moment when nothing happened, he had to take pity on the children.

"Down, children."

There were various noises of relief, then awe as Berlush started to uncoil directly up into the air. After a few minutes he hung there, a cart length from the ground, with nothing to support him and no signs of effort. His great head turned toward where the children were gathering around Cherale.

"My thanks, schoolteacher. My thanks, blacksmith."

He swept a long pass around the field before returning to hover over the children, his length disguised on the complex shifting coils he wove in the air: "Thank you, children. Without your help I would surely have died."

He extended himself slowly and drifted over to Cherale and Robert.

"I am indebted to you both. If you should need help from the high skies, scatter fennel in your forge for a night and one of mine will find me, if I do not sense your call directly."

With that, he spun a dizzying whirl of intertwined shapes before shooting straight up into the sky with a roar that only faded as he vanished through the clouds. Robert smiled as he looked at Cherale and her class, rooted to the spot and still staring open mouthed at where Berlush had disappeared. He had to clap his hands to get their attention: "Now children, if anyone asks you, today in class Miss Lorris had asked me to visit and demonstrate how the big haywain wheels were lifted. This was to show you how many little things are able to lift big things. Because nobody will believe we lifted a dragon up so it could fly again, would they?"

***

A WINTER AT COURT

*A tale from the realm of Khyr. This one from
one of the capital cities in that mythical land.*

During the summer, the court at Parthienne was a scintillating place to be: the sunlight through the stained glass windows, the scent of blossoms on the plants and trees throughout the grounds, the swirling capes of the courtiers, the elaborate dresses of the ladies.

But in the winter, the court took upon itself a very different hue: the dull tones of the rain on the windows, the deep browns of the bare earth and the skeletal trees in the grounds. The courtiers and their ladies went away, the fortunate to the Winter Palace in the south, the out of favour to their family demesnes; no matter how gay for the year's end festivals, dreary in comparison to what they were missing. Or so the few unlucky servants left to maintain the dismal, echoing edifice thought.

*

Agnes shuffled slowly down the musty corridor, the bucket of grey liquid that had been water getting heavier with every tired step. Every year it was the same, the overseer who was picked to lead the winter maintenance staff treating it as a death sentence and taking out his or her frustrations on everyone who answered to him or her. This year it was Dolores, a woman so rotund and prone to inactivity that the staff referred to her as 'The Barrel' when she was out of hearing range, which was often.

Agnes paused in her travail as again she caught the faintest strains of music. That was three nights running. Where could it be coming from? The court was closed, the instruments gone away with their owners to the Winter Palace. She turned slowly, regarding the grey stone walls and pale cream flagstones dimly gleaming in the glow of the torch that illumined the junction far behind her. The place would be a lot less gloomy, Agnes thought, if the cressets were all lit. The faintest sounds of melody came again and she decided that this mystery would not persist for another night. Putting her mop and bucket next to a grand display of the late Duke's ceremonial armour, she set off quietly, pausing frequently to listen for the elusive sounds.

She wandered several corridors, becoming aware that her path led towards the great ballroom. She moved carefully, her years dropping from her as curiosity took over. After some while, she arrived at the doors of the great hall, and sure enough, the melody came from within. It was a strange tune, a lilting air that made her want to grab a partner and whirl a stately, graceful reel like those her late husband had delighted in. She shook her head. Tom was twenty years gone, taken in one of the interminable battles the old Duke had insisted kept the blood of his men strong. He had been delivered back to her on a cart and had gasped his last words through a bloody froth as he bled all over her best shawl.

"I love you, Agnes Forster. You could have had any man, but you chose me. Thank-"

She took a deep, calming breath and reached for the door handle. With a rush, she twisted, pushed and entered as soon as the gap was wide enough to admit her.

The great ballroom stood empty, its chandeliers covered in drapes and portraits looking down at the vast expanse of polished oak parquet flooring. The room was dim with shadows and her breathing echoed in the silence. She looked about and saw no-one. She was just turning to go when her eyes fell on the shadows on the opposite wall. There were too many. She stared. The shadows were of a group of people standing as if regarding her. She crossed herself, something she had not done for years. With that, the shadows moved as if retreating. She felt a hand fall on her shoulder and she shrieked. A calming voice with an unfamiliar accent spoke by her ear.

"Please don't do that, it makes us uncomfortable."

Agnes stared about, but the touch on her shoulder had no hand and the owner of the voice was nowhere to be seen. She cried out in a quavering voice, "Show yourselves. This is no way to treat a poor cleaning woman. I danced in here in my youth, I'll have you know."

There was a chuckle behind her: "Indeed you did, Agnes de Montecour. Such a brave decision, to marry for love and put aside the rich future your family had lined up for you."

Agnes started. She had not been called that since her eighteenth birthday. "I am Agnes Forster, and proud of that. De Montecour was lost to me a long time ago."

"Indeed. Would you dance again, Agnes Forster?"

Agnes paused. Now she was calmer, she got no shivers from this shadow host. She'd always know the presence of evil from her family gift. Whatever this was, it was nothing of the dark. She smiled. "I'm not so spry anymore, but I'll accept your noble offer, good sir."

The laughter was like water chimes as a voice far away cried words she did not recognise:

"Deonaigh amharc."

With a silent explosion, the grand ballroom transformed itself like a carpet of colour being unrolled. The chandeliers took on a sparkling radiance with little winged figures cavorting about them. The walls were hung with elaborate drapes worked in silver and gold filigree. The shadows on the walls linked themselves to the host of tall, slim folk with flowing robes, fantastical dresses, pale complexions, hair in every colour imaginable and worn long, either loose or braided. The entire host regarded her with angular eyes that ran the full spectrum of shades of violet. But it was their delicately pointed ears gave them away to Agnes.

"Sidhe." She whispered it in awe as the owner of the voice stepped from behind her, his deep blue, burgundy and purple formal dress exaggerating his pale complexion and yellow eyes. Silver hair hung to his waist. He bowed almost to the floor, a full formal greeting with the swirling wrist flourish so difficult to achieve without looking effeminate. He did it perfectly.

"You honour me, Lady Agnes. I am Danruben of the Gilded Tower, Master at Arms to the Elfire Court. These luminaries opposite are the scion of that vaunted estate."

Agnes could not help blushing as his effusive greeting woke memories of a teenage child of nobility and wealth. She extended her hand: "Sir Danruben, I am delighted to make your acquaintance. Shall we step a reel together to see how we fit?"

Danruben smiled and took her hand, then stepped in close to place a hand on the small of her back. "I think that would be splendid. Let us reel."

And reel they did, many times. Agnes laughed as the ceiling seemed to spin faster than she did while the glorious host turned and turned about in the curlicues of the dances. After an interminable time, she placed a hand on Danruben's chest and called a halt. He escorted her to one side and plied her with a heady golden wine that she could taste the very sunlight in. She took only two sips before turning to him.

"This is all well and good, Sir Danruben, but what of this disporting in the Duke's court while he is away?"

Danruben smiled. "T'was a bargain struck with the present Duke's great-grandmother. She was gifted far more than that line usually received, and saw the shades of discontent and malfeasance that brooded in the corners of the empty court, growing stronger as time passed and eventually reaching a point where they could leap to human hosts. It is a curse of old buildings where strong emotions are played out. So she used her knowledge to make an offer to the Elfire Court. For the winter, we could revel here, taking up the essences of the worldly court for our enrichment and in so doing, blight the growth of the shades."

Agnes was impressed. Her mother had always said that the old dowager had been a gifted sorceress. She looked about the ballroom with its graceful dancers, then returned her attention back to Danruben.

"That explains you and here. What about me?"

Danruben bowed his head. "Forgive me. It was an indulgence of mine that was granted as my year gift from the scions of Elfire."

Agnes regarded him coolly. "An indulgence? I feel a better explanation is in order, sir."

Danruben took her hands in his, noting the slender fingers with their calluses from years of hard labour accepted as a penalty for the warmth of love.

"We are long lived, Agnes. I saw you on the day you were introduced to court. I thought you pretty but unfortunately another spoiled noble brat. Three years later your beauty had grown, but your maturity and rejection of a life of ease for love took my breath away. I did not know it then, but I had become smitten with you. So I looked for you as the years passed, occasionally seeing you from afar as the grounds and the town beyond are anathema to my kind. I heard of your husband's passing, a petty revenge wreaked by your father: although you only suspected, I knew. Since then, I have been here every winter, watching you drudge for the uncaring, your slender beauty enduring all that they burden you with. Upon this season, my naming time came around again as it does every century of your years. For my gift, I asked for the chance to offer you a love and a life like you have never known."

He sat there, his heart in his eyes as Agnes' world shattered and was reformed in a moment of vertigo and grief. She raised a hand to his face.

"I am near done, dear elf. My years are many."

Danruben placed his hand over hers and smiled again. "T'would be a poor name season gift if it did not have the longevity of its recipient, now wouldn't it?"

Agnes shook her head. This was a little too much. Danruben caught her chin in his other hand. He looked her straight in the eyes.

"I am not asking for your love. I am offering you an extended life away from the toils you have endured, to finally have the adventures of youth with the eyes and mind of maturity."

Agnes sat. She thought of Dolores the Barrel and then of her own little bare room in the cellar of the keep. She looked at the wedding band on her finger. With a trembling hand, she took it off and set it on the window ledge. Tom would understand. He always had understood her so much better than she had understood herself. She turned to Danruben and his pensive look made her decision easier.

"Let us dance some more, Sir Danruben. I do believe I am free for the next season or two."

Danruben laughed long with joy and so did she, and that easy laughter became their trademark in the Sidhe courts as they had many a grand adventure.

***

GEYLON AND THE GREEN GIRL

A tale from the past of 'These Pagan Isles' - a Britain not quite as mundane as history would have us believe.

The first telling of this tale occurred at the planting of the first sacred grove on the Sussex Downs in several centuries.

Geylon stood upon the hill as the fires burned for their second night. Water and fire versus earth he thought, as the dull thud of mallets on wood foretold the demise of another stone beyond the circle of firelight below. Another heathen temple destroyed by the might of Rome. Geylon looked out across the little valley, to the forest beyond. Heathen it may be, but it was a beautiful land, as verdant as it was ancient.

His musings were interrupted by a tugging on his trews, down by his knee. Geylon started and looked down. Standing by him was a little winged figure dressed in a silken wrap of forest green hues, her pale jade complexion glistening with diamond clear tears wept from deep emerald eyes.

"Why do they break the circle?" she asked in a plaintive voice.

Geylon stood, struck dumb in wonder and the faintest twinge of fear.

"Without that, I cannot go home. I will dwell here and get heavier and heavier, then I won't be able to fly, then I won't remember where I came from, then I won't remember at all. Why are they doing this?"

Geylon felt his soul shrink as her delicate wings drooped in dejection. He sat cross legged, after looking quickly about to make sure that the centurion was not around.

"They do this to banish the old gods from this land, so a new god can come and make the people happy."

"But what about the people that don't want a new god? I don't want any god who burns trees to break stones."

Geylon sighed. The little winged one had a point. His father had been a carpenter, working only with wood that the forest yielded to him. His father had taken to the woods when the priest arrived in town, pausing only to curse the day that a fellow woodworker decided he had a divine parent and a mission. The green girl cried, and Geylon made his decision.

"They broke your ring of stones in ignorance and fear. I'll rebuild it with knowledge, but you'll have to help me with that."

She looked up at him through a mist of tears. Then grinned: "How can you promise when you can't even lift a bit of one of the stones?"

Geylon hated moments like this. Then he grinned right back: "Stones. Can't lift stones. Can't grow them either. But what about trees?"

Her saddened face lit up as she uttered a joyous cry: "Acorns!"

So when the legion finally left Brittania, Geylon took his leave and made his way back to the valley where the green girl waited. Renewing his promise, he cleared the ruined circle, and in each crater left by a stone, he planted an acorn, washed with his blood and her tears. Then the waiting began.

Geylon journeyed to find work and gain a feel for the land and its people. The green girl waited, dancing the sabbat and esbat festivals around the ring, binding the trees to be with the echoes of the riven stones.

*

Geylon's travels took him far, and further still with the coming of the low kings, who ruled that all the land was property and as such had to have an owner. So after many years Geylon returned to the valley and set to work for the local king as a bard, tutor and guardian to his sons. Always he returned to the stones and always the green girl flitted from the moonlit trees to greet him, despairing at his greying hair, not really understanding the concept of age. But both took a childish delight in the saplings growth, far quicker than oaks in less favoured soil.

"It's the stones." she explained. "They want to be again. And form is not a matter for ancient earth."

Geylon wondered, at these moments, whether his painstaking learning really meant anything at all. He always left the stones more sprightly than when he arrived, but he never noticed. The green girl had thought hard about that, and with a little weaving of the moon she took his age, which did him no good, and passed it to the oaks, which did them good.

Years passed and finally the king came to a moment he had dreaded ever since his sons had become men. Their beloved Geylon was leaving, and after such sterling service, it was meet that the king should grant him a request. These could be ruinous. So when the quiet voiced tutor merely asked for the rights to the little valley at the far end of his fief, although in perpetuity, he was overcome with relief. Geylon left with papers granting him eternal right to the valley in his satchel. Ownership? Ridiculous. He would be the valley's custodian to the end of his days. Then it would be left alone, as it should have been all those years before.

So Geylon returned to the valley to stay, and built himself a basic dwelling, half in the earth for strength. With the green girl's help he lived sparsely, learning much of the ways of the forest and it's folk. As the trees grew, wrapping their roots tighter about the riven stones below, so Geylon listened to the green girl's tales of home, her morning land of beauty and magic. He even joined in her festival dances, finding them strangely beneficial. But his favourite pastime was to listen and watch as the green girl told of her Lady, she who made them all, Seelie and Unseelie, she who walked their land and watched over his. The green girl's descriptions surpassed Geylon's senses, leaving images of grace and power in his mind's eye.

Meanwhile, the lonely god grew in power across the land, but not as much as his followers did. This led to competition to be noticed, and thus the devout did go forth to seek out the devil's work in all its forms and destroy them. One young priest and his retinue sojourned at a tavern in the king's fief, and heard a tale of a mad hermit who had made a circle of oaks grow overnight to replace a stone circle. This was more like it! Filled with fervour, the priest and his escort set off next morning to put an end to this heathen witch.

They ploughed through the forest as they couldn't find the trail that the villagers had told of. The going was heavy, with every bush and branch seemingly out to hinder their progress. After two days of being whipped, tripped and tangled by what was purported to be pleasant woodland, the priest decided that one crazy old man and his stone fixation was not a menace to believers anyway. He led his group back to the village, not noting the ease of their passage out of the woodland that had been so difficult to travel into.

Many decades had passed since the night that Geylon had stood on a hill and looked down on burning stones. The years between had been filled with experiences, but most of all, the green girl's bright company. Geylon now realised how much his promise would cost him when the revived circle allowed the green girl a way home. But he had promised to make good the vandalism of his fellows, and he would keep his word.

At the winter solstice, Geylon's age passed a point where the faerie glamours of the green girl could sustain him. She begged him come into the circle to rest, that he may see a last dance. As the green girl wove a slightly sadder dance around the stones, Geylon looked up at the stars above and made a wish: "Let this bright child find her way home. If it take my death to finish my work, let it be so."

The green girl stopped, and Geylon watched as the stars seemed to tumble from the heavens to form a lattice between the westernmost trunks. The lattice shifted, whirled and opened. Wisps of mist drifted through from a twilit meadow that lay beyond. With a cry of joy the green girl arrowed between the oaks and was gone across the meadow. Geylon felt his heart slump. Not even a farewell. He felt his years, and smiled. Time for him to go home. He closed his eyes and lay back, content.

A tugging on his trews, down by the knee, brought him back. The green girl stood, a latent smile playing about her lips. She saw she had his attention, then flew to land on the shoulder of the figure in the gateway. Geylon blinked and then the breath froze in his chest as a hand gloved in silver lace lifted. Pale hair drifted in a breeze unfelt as a voice that exceeded his imaginings called to him: "You have returned one of my children. You have righted a wrong to this land. You have given your life that she may live. Yet you do not even know her name. For that, take her hand and come away, come away."

The mist faded and the stars shone down, and the oak grove was still.

***

SPRING MEL⊕DY

~ The Wheel of the Year; Awakening ~

A tale from the today of 'These Pagan Isles' - a Britain not quite as mundane as some would have us believe.

Steve pondered, as he regarded the gravel adjacent to him, if he would ever get the hang of remembering that he could not hold his drink after he had started drinking. His rebellious stomach had reminded him with its usual hour of misery, and he now lay where his friends had left him, face down on the grass verge outside the pub. From within came the sounds of a serious party, which he had again tried to be the heart and soul of and again found himself reduced to sick spectatorship.

He rolled over, slid down the slope and then carefully sat up. His head was worryingly clear, which meant he was in for an Olympic standard hangover after he finally got some rest. That would be tomorrow. Or was it today? After Jerry had come storming in, ranting of another wild party, time had become irrelevant. Why he fell for Jerry's garbled English exhortations every time he never knew, but off they went again and here he was again, watching the outside of a party. The outside of a party was always depressing; he mused, then shook his head to break the impending maudlin mood and immediately regretted the sudden movement. After his head stopped spinning, he sat back up and took stock of his surroundings while gathering himself to return to the fray. His resigned glance stopped at a movement in the shadows of the big tree that loomed over the car park. Like a little flag. He squinted, forcing his blurred vision to focus. No, not a flag. The bottom of a skirt, where it draped a possibly slim form leaning on the tree. Another casualty of the party? A lady in distress? The night was looking up.

Steve's progress across the car park was hindered by cars getting in the way like wayward dogs after a fuss, or so it seemed. Yet again, He swore under his breath: "Not another drop. Uncle Alcohol and I are no longer related."

Finally he reached the shadows under the tree. Bloody big one too, he thought. He started as the woman, no, girl, turned green eyes that seemed to catch the moonlight toward him. Be casual thought Steve, be real cool.

"Hi. You okay? Needed a little air after the lasht dansh, huh?" Oh god, he thought, my mouth's under the control of a drunken idiot.

"I'm fine, but why are you so lonely?" Her voice was soft and lilting. Her words may as well have been body blows. Steve sat down suddenly as blood rushed into his head with a roar. Lonely! How did she know? One of the boys was Steve. Never missed a soccer match did Steve. Smooth Steve, never kept a girl long, lucky bloke.

Steve who watched the full moon rise every month, struck by a distant longing that drove him to take refuge in whiskey before sleep would come. Steve who watched old friends, strangers now, with women he had never met, sharing moments he had never had. Steve the lad who wanted nothing more than - what? He realised that he had not the faintest idea. He unconsciously wiped away the tears that had started unnoticed and looked up at the girl.

"Am I lonely?"

"You are, but you aren't. You just don't understand."

"What? Understand what?"

"The way things work for folk of your blood, the ca-"

"Yo Steve!"

From a range of almost ten feet, Jerry bellowed cheerfully before taking another look at Steve's companion.

"'Allo darlin'. Wotcha hangin' with niceboy for? Got loadsa fings we can do..."

Jerry's leer should have split his face in two. Would have, if Steve had been standing up.

"I'm quite happy here with -" She paused and looked down. "What did you say your name was?"

"Steve."

"I'm going for a walk with Steve. So you'll just have to do 'things' on your own."

"Not likely, sugarlips! Come 'ere!"

Jerry made a grab for her arm, and Steve fell over as he tried to get up to stop him. As his head bounced off the wing of a parked car, his vision went to little bright pieces, alternating reality with random colours and bits of fantasy. His sight caught images of the car park, the girl, Jerry, the big bloke with the horned hat, the tree, the gravel, the pub and then the girl was leaning over him again.

"While you were resting, your friend went back inside. Walk with me?"

Steve heaved a sigh of relief. Jerry had relented for once, must remember to buy him a beer tomorrow. He nodded and stood up shakily, noticing the patch of fluid by the tree as they walked away. Funny how beer always looked so dark when it was spilt, he thought. Then he felt a slender arm slip through his and he forgot all about it.

They walked for a while in silence as Steve gradually got himself together. She seemed to sense this, humming a cheerful tune that Steve could not quite put a name to. As he recovered, he noticed that the pub was nowhere in sight. The woodland about was thicker than he had ever seen before, but then again, when had he last been in the woods? Oh yes, Aunt Elizabeth's funeral, where as a boy, he'd walked proudly carrying a little branch off a big tree. He had watched with mild curiosity as the family from 'Aunt Lizzie's side' silently buried her in quiet woodland to the muttered disapproval of Aunt Dorothy, a devout churchgoer. She was responsible for his Sunday school attendance and subsequent loathing of things religious.

"Steve."

Her voice snapped him out of his reverie. They stood in a shadowed glade, the full moon barely visible through the arching boughs above. With a shock, Steve recognised this place. He turned to the woman, numbed to the core: "This place... Aunt Elizabeth's grave. How did you know? What are you trying to do? Hell! Who on earth are you?"

She smiled. Lovely, he thought, then broke the distraction by shaking his head again. She was still smiling. She knew the effect her smile had. Damn.

"Hmmm, lots of questions. I knew your Aunt. To wake you up. I'm not entirely of that earth."

"How did you know - Hang on! *That* earth?"

"Yes." The grin was beautiful. More mischief had been bred from that grin than any Sidhe prank. How did he know that? Sidhe? Whoa! Steve stepped back and gasped for air. Meanwhile, she sat down cross-legged on the grass.

"Slowly, lady. Very slowly."

"All right, man. I knew your aunt, just as I know all who work my ways. I even met her, once or twice. She said to me, on the last time we met,

'That lad, he'll need guiding iffen he gets lost. But he'll come true. Give him a secret and he'll come true.' "

Her voice had imitated Aunt Lizzie's perfectly. So perfectly that Steve had to sit down as well. With a quick grin she reached out a hand and closed his mouth, stroking his jaw as she pulled her hand back.

"Your aunt was a one, and she tricked me into promising to guide you. It's not often I get tricked, not without wanting to be, that is."

"That earth?"

"You're not in the apparent world. Your aunt's grave was lost there years ago, but I pulled it through here to keep it safe. This is the awakened land, the morning time, and I needed it here so when I brought you here I could fulfil my promise."

"What promise?"

The creak of leather behind Steve was the only warning he had.

"To wake you up, Harbinger of Spring."

The deep, resonant voice emanated from just by his left ear and he leapt high into the air to land in a tumble of limbs and little surprised cries that turned to laughter. Steve choked on his outraged cry as the owner of the voice became clear through a blizzard of gossamer wings and svelte green bodies. They settled to form a miniature host sitting in the horns of the glowing eyed being that lay comfortably, head supported on one heavily muscled arm. Its lambent yellow eyes regarded him without blink or pupils. The massive shock took Steve to semi-consciousness as his blood thundered in his ears. Distantly he heard three knocks, rolling like thunder across unknown skies.

In a gentle voice she said, "It is done. My thanks for this, horned one. I know my presence disturbs you at this time."

"Disturb does not come close."

The wry humour of the remark awakened Steve. Knowledge came unbidden. They had known each other for ages, comfortable in a love that surpassed creation. He sat up, his head clear. She smiled. From within the trees, the horned being nodded once before moving silently away.

"Um."

She laughed, and the clearing blossomed. Clouds of Thanna Sidhe danced frenzied flights of delight as her laughter shook Spring from its lair. Steve gasped. He knew that the little sprites were Thanna Sidhe. Faeriekin. Her laughter faded but she looked at him with laughter still in her eyes.

"Oh my, the chosen one quoth 'Um'."

"Lady, he's only a mortal. And one of the modern breeds too."

This from a tall, elegantly garbed being with white hair, pointed ears and violet eyes. Steve recognised a pureblood Sidhe, using newborn knowledge still uncomfortable in his mind.

"Your arrogance ill becomes you."

Her admonition grounded the flyers. With murmurs of consternation, they hid amidst the lush grasses.

"I am merely pointing out that the trace of fey that runs in some of the mortal blood lines is getting a little thin, by all evidence."

"Go. Now. You will not abuse my affection for your race to hurl insults at a guest."

The tall figure lurched as if struck, then spun gracefully and departed swiftly. The girl turned back, all traces of imperiousness gone. Little faces peered around clumps of grasses. She sighed.

"Ever the weakness of the head clans, arrogance. But enough. You have a promise to help me keep."

Steve warily eyed the turquoise impette that was playing cat's cradle with his shoelaces.

"Promise?"

"Faerie promises. Complex things. A promise to help another promise to be fulfilled. In so doing, I find myself having to promise that I'll guide you so that your aunt's promise to me can be completed. Tricky one, your aunt. Brilliant at faerie intrigue. Few mortals are."

"So what do I do?"

"Be yourself."

That grin again.

"Stop trying to fit in. Follow your heart. Walk out under that moon you pine over. Dance for her. Listen to her. Learn from her."

"My moon. You know."

"She and I are one. I am flattered."

Steve's knowledge settled. He winced, blushed crimson, stood up, then knelt before her.

"Lady. I have walked with a goddess and talked nonsense. Forgive me."

"Nought to forgive. Will you walk in my ways, and bring my ways to those who seek?"

"When I have learned of them, yes."

"Then go as a man, not priest nor preacher. They are not welcome in my realms."

"Your realms?"

"Anywhere where my names have been called, be it room or garden, forest or field."

"I understand, a little. I will understand more. Thank you."

"Time to go."

She waved her hand in a graceful dismissal. Steve was preparing to rise when the clearing fell in on him with a screech. Green mushroomed in his view as fey laughter spun his senses into numbness. Through the green chaos, a lilting voice followed him down.

"Awake, my harbinger, awake for summer is near, but not come. Be the promise of burgeoning life for all who need it. Be yourself. Shed the chrysalis of soul's winter and join the dancing folk. They dance in every land and you will know them, and find friends. But bring her to them as well. You will know her more."

The lilt turned to command: "Like mist in the sun, the veil is lifted."

Steve saw himself, dusty and damp, walking up to a girl in jeans and an enormous sweatshirt. She was covered in dust and grease with a dirty car behind her. Then the mist came back down, and Steve landed hard.

He picked himself up and looked about. A country road, miles from anywhere. He sighed and stuck his hands in his pockets as he started to wander down the road. He'd just convinced himself that he had to try that beer again when a packet dropped at his feet, neatly wrapped in a piece of delicate cloth, held by a ribbon of intricately woven snowdrops. He picked it up and walked on, looking about. A smile lit his face. As he undid the ribbon, the snowdrops drifted to the roadside, taking root. Little wings flapped and faded. As he unwrapped the cloth, it fluttered in the sun before unravelling into mist. Inside was his wallet. A voice in his ear whispered.

"A promise kept. Now keep one for me. Pass the awakening on. Bring spring to the souls in winter. Carry the fire within and share it with those who seek. They each have the spark inside and you can fan it to flame. You can learn from each other, as well as from the spirits. Like sunlight upon the mist, this light reveals."

Putting his wallet away, Steve sauntered down the road, humming a tune he had heard somewhere.

*

Allison dried her tears. Bloody car! Middle of nowhere all night, missed the damn party, nearly froze, nothing to look forward to before Monday. She settled to doze a while in the sun before walking back to town. A faint tune ceasing caught her attention. A diffident voice made her jump:

"Um, Hi. Need a hand?"

***

SUMMER MADRIGAL

~ The Wheel of the Year; Searching ~

*A tale from the today of 'These Pagan Isles' - a Britain
not quite as mundane as some would have us believe.*

The stones seemed to stand uncaring as the reverent and the revelling performed their various solstice rituals. Karen moved among them, looking for the same thing she did every year: her year king, her dark man of the woods. She knew he was here. All she had to do was keep looking. One solstice they would meet, and...

What?

Karen's vision had never gone beyond their meeting, the crowds around going wild as the dawn rose, his brown eyes gazing warmly into hers, his beard neat, his clothing soft under her hands. His smile revealed even white teeth, his breath sweet with a hint of coffee and mint.

She moved into one of those sudden open spaces that the eddies of a crowd can spontaneously create. But this clearing had a reason. On the ground in front of her a man lay cradled in the arms of a little girl, a wheelchair tipped over behind them. Wondering but strangely uncaring glances flitted across them from the crowd as it flowed around. Karen sighed as her training rose to the fore. She moved up to them and crouched down by the girl.

"Hi. My name's Karen, I'm a nurse. What's your name?"

The girl turned her head in Karen's direction, eyes of palest green flecked with gold, unseeing.

"My name is Callie-Anne and I don't see properly. This is my daddy, his name is Malcolm and he's very sick. Grandpa always says he shouldn't come."

"Where's your Mummy, Callie-Anne?"

"Mummy is in the Summerlands and Daddy says that she will always be there to watch over me."

Karen shook herself back from the strange place that Callie-Anne's words had sent her to. In the warm dawn light, a chill crossed her as she checked

Malcolm over. Callie-Anne and her Grandpa were right. Daddy was very sick and shouldn't have come.

It took Karen nearly twenty minutes to get help and get Malcolm to the St John Ambulance who were thankfully as efficient as ever. Within moments of her arriving and describing Malcolm's condition, an air ambulance was on the way to meet the St John staff in a nearby field. Throughout this, Callie-Anne had a hand fisted around Karen's belt and kept pace with her. After ensuring that Malcolm would be comfortable, Karen looked down at the girl.

"Your Daddy is going to have to go to hospital. Can your Grandpa come and take you or should I get a police lady to go with you?"

Callie-Anne fished around in her pocket for a moment before extracting a battered business card and handing it to Karen.

"My Grandpa said I should always carry this and not tell Daddy. If Daddy got in trouble, I should give it to the person who wanted to help me and mentioned the police."

Karen took the card, vague misgivings starting to circle her mind. The card was plain but had been printed a long time ago on very high quality stock. The embossing was lost to time and creases, but the name and hand written phone number with an appended central London dial code were easily read:

Jonathan Marduke Thomas

She pulled out her mobile and entered the number. It rang once. A distinguished, quiet voice replied.

"Where did he collapse?"

Karen started, then gathered herself.

"I am afraid your son collapsed at Stonehenge and is being airlifted to –"

"No destinations please, madam. I presume his daughter is with you?"

"Yes."

"Then a car will be with you momentarily. Would you please agree to accompany her to the hospital? I shall meet you there and happily make it worth your while."

Karen paused, then the curiosity that her father had always said would be the death of her won out.

"Of course. How will I know the car?"

"It will be big and green and she will know it."

"Alright. I look forward to meeting you."

"And I you, madam."

Callie-Anne looked up at Karen.

"He's sending the car?"

"Yes."

"Oh good. I like Mandrake."

"Is that the car's name?"

"No silly. Mandrake is the driver."

Karen went to the car-park exit nearest the road with Callie-Anne to wait as the helicopter with her father disappeared into the distance. The car arrived within half an hour, a Range Rover that made almost no noise. The driver was dressed in a quality pale suit but his manner allowed him to pass through the dispersing revellers with a minimum of derision and delay.

"Miss Queen, a sad pleasure to see you again."

"Oh, hello Mandrake. Can we go fast please? This is Karen and she's a nurse and she helped Daddy when no-one else would."

Mandrake's grey eyes met Karen's.

"A pleasure indeed. Ladies, shall we away?"

Karen's first thought on entering the car was that there was some very serious money involved somewhere. The car was rolling luxury, with suspension that just made road irregularities vanish. Within ten minutes, she and Callie-Anne were playing some ridiculous computer game involving exploding flowers on the screen set in the back of the driver's seat, while Mandrake piloted the vehicle at an obscene speed through the light morning traffic. It was at least half an hour before Karen looked up and did not recognise any of the landscape passing by at speed.

"I though we were going to the hospital?"

Mandrake and Callie-Anne replied in chorus: "We are. It's a special hospital."

Karen was alarmed until she caught Mandrake looking at her in the driver's mirror.

"Don't worry, Miss. Malcolm is far better being treated at the facility that knows his illness. It's quite close now."

The car sped on for a few more minutes before making a sharp turn. Karen recognised the landmark in the distance. Silbury Hill. They were miles from anywhere with the advanced medical facilities Malcolm had so plainly needed. The car slowed rapidly and turned again to descend an earthen ramp into a torchlit chamber. Figures in white robes moved about with purpose as the car came to a silent stop. Callie-Anne leapt from the car.

"Come on Karen. Grandpa should be here by now."

He was. Jonathan Thomas was a grey bearded giant of a man dressed in spotless Armani. He strode forward to sweep Callie-Anne into a huge laughing hug before putting her down, taking her hand and walking at Callie-Anne's pace up to Karen. He extended his hand.

"Thank you, madam."

Karen was a little flustered and resorted to her best bedside manner.

"It was no problem, Mister Thomas. I just hope we got Malcolm here in time."

Jonathan smiled.

"You did indeed."

Karen detected additional meaning in his reply and smile. She decided that it was time to get some answers.

"Could you explain to me how a mortally ill patient was allowed to go to a festival that would plainly threaten his life?"

Jonathan looked startled and Callie-Anne replied.

"Daddy always goes to Stonehenge for the solstice. It's more of a problem if he doesn't because he can't die right."

Karen took a step back. Surely the girl hadn't said that? Jonathan glanced down at Callie-Anne and gently shook her hand back and forth.

"Young lady, you know that is rude and yet you always do it."

Callie-Anne grinned impudently up at him.

"It saves time, Grandpa. She came to him. She was looking for him. If she can't handle the end she won't be able to cope with the beginning. It's quicker this way."

Jonathan stared at Callie-Anne, then his face relaxed into a smile. He looked up at Karen.

"Would a drink and an explanation be appropriate about now?"

Karen gathered herself and looked about. The robed figures were not medical staff. They seemed to be some sort of religious order. Druids? She looked back at Jonathan.

"A stiff drink would be a very good idea. Then you can explain this mystery to me."

A little while later, they were all sat in very comfortable chairs in a curtained-off alcove on one side of the chamber. Karen had sunk a large schnapps and was just starting on a black coffee. Callie-Anne sat quietly and Jonathan waited.

Karen gathered her scattered thoughts. "What the hell is going on here?"

Jonathan leant back and stared at the ceiling. "I presume that you are pagan in your general beliefs?"

"Yes."

"Then you are familiar with the concept of the year-king, the chosen one who lived as royalty for a year before being sacrificed to ensure the good of the land?"

"Yes."

"Then permit me to embroider upon your understanding. The practice of sacrificing the year-king goes back a long way. But here in the shire of the great circles, it was deemed to be too costly after a plague decimated the people in the South of Albion. So a pact was struck, and a year king came forth from the earth hereabouts. The locals at the time built a mound over the spot to commemorate the event. Being of Gaelic origin, they called the place Sil-ri, the 'king-seep', the spot where the year king seeped from the ground. This year king was different. Providing he had a consort, every harvest he would waste away to seep from the ground again at the Winter Solstice, being reborn. In many ways, a reinforcement of the wheel of the year rather than a deviation. He chose his look on his first incarnation and up until seven years ago, he died and returned annually on the top of Silbury Hill, ably warded and honoured by a distaff branch of the Ancient Order of Druids. But seven years ago, Callie-Anne's mother, his consort of twenty years, was run down by a drunk driver as she visited Avebury. He has not been able to go properly, and has lingered in this wasted state since then, only insisting that he visit Stonehenge for the Summer Solstice because there was a lady looking for him."

Karen looked up from her glass, eyes almost glowing in the diffuse light: "Take me to him."

Jonathan nodded and Callie-Anne sprang forward to take Karen's hand. She whispered, "I told them you felt right."

Karen walked across the chamber, her insides quivering and her mind spinning as it tried to get a grip on what was happening. In a dimly-lit room, Malcolm lay with his head and upper body raised. He smiled with a ruined grin as she entered. Karen ignored everything except his eyes. She placed her hands on either side of his head and stared deep into his brown eyes. The palsied body and rotted teeth were immaterial if her year king was wasted for lack of his consort. But his eyes would match her lifelong dream. She stared hard into his eyes and the room span. Deep within those eyes she saw recognition. She felt his breath catch as lightning flashed from his brow to hers. Three dull paeans of thunder echoed through the chamber. Shaking, she held on to him through them as her limbs turned to fire and her core to ice. This was him. He was sick with need for her. But not for long. Harvest time was approaching, and he would return to the earth, and at Winter Solstice, she would finally meet him. Next summer solstice, they would stand as her dream dictated and something wonderful would happen afterwards. She felt Callie-Anne touch her neck and whisper in her ear,

"Then I'll have a sister."

Malcolm smiled.

***

AUTUMN RHYTHM

~ The Wheel of the Year; Releasing ~

*A tale from the today of 'These Pagan Isles' - a Britain
not quite as mundane as some would have us believe.*

Sally cried as the fire died and shadows shrouded the bottles and cans strewn about the circle. Down in the quarry the last light did not penetrate, and even the wind seemed reluctant to intrude on her vigil. Another ruined meeting, another night smarting over the drunken ridicule heaped on her life. Why did they even bother to come? Why did she bother to bring them? Because she had to. Because sometimes, just sometimes, when they'd had just enough to drink, they actually got into the coven thing and the circle glowed in her sight, and she got fleeting glimpses of movement at the edges of her vision. But the sometimes were getting rarer. She never drank on craft nights and this was probably the root of some of the trouble. The drunken camaraderie shared by the rest of them meant that she stood alone, even though she drank after the working.

With a sigh she gave up her contemplations and rummaged in her bag. Down past the incense and candles, the tarot deck and athame, she found the final piece of ritual gear. Shaking open the bin liner, she started her regular task of clearing the ground. As she worked her thoughts turned again to the futility of it all. Teenage witches, yeah right. Given the evidence about her, the parental factions could hardly be blamed for calling it all an excuse to party under the stars.

"Party! Damnitall, there's more serious things to be done out here," she muttered as another bottle joined the growing legion in the bag. She stopped her picking as something crunched under someone else's foot. Probably the remains of a bag of crisps reduced to crumbs; the random thought diverted on her alarm. She straightened up, looking warily about as she retreated to her bag. A figure stood in the shadows between her and the path out of the quarry. Not good. She knelt and felt around in the bag for her other knife, the one the coven knew nothing about, whilst never taking her eyes from the shadowed intruder.

"Good evening, my dear."

A deep voice, but calming. The figure stepped forward into the tiny pool of light shed by the waning fire. Sally sighed. The old geezer wouldn't be a menace if she didn't let him near.

"Just clearing up after the party. I'll be gone in a few minutes."

"Looks like the remains of an autumnal rite ruined by a coven of sceptical drunkards to me."

Sally froze, knife forgotten. The old man smiled. "Don't mind me m'dear, I've been watching witches in this hole in the ground for longer than you'd believe."

"Ah. Um. Well, I'll still be gone in a few minutes. Didn't realise that the quarry was under guard. We'll not be back again."

With that sentence, Sally realised that she'd made a decision. The coven, for what it was worth, was history.

"Yes, autumn is a time for shedding cover and facing the cold alone, ready to grow again."

Sally stared, puzzled by the comment.

"What?"

The old man smiled as he moved to sit against the great boulder that spoiled the quarry's smooth curve. He produced a bottle from his satchel.

"Wine?"

He waved the bottle in her direction as his other hand produced two small cups from somewhere. He stood and poured himself a cup, before stepping forward and placing the bottle and cup on the ground between Sally and himself. He then returned to his impromptu seat.

"Do have a drink m'dear, and I'll expound a little on the previous sentence."

Sally hesitated, then crouched and poured herself a cup. Which she swilled about and threw on the ground before pouring herself another.

"Do you always libate before drinking? Must make a nasty mess at home." He smiled as he finished speaking.

"Just flushing out any sleepy stuff, and the name's Sally, not m'dear." He looked startled then nodded his head.

"Fair enough. Being offered drinks by a stranger in a nighted quarry should warrant some caution."

Sally perched herself on the upturned crate that had served as an altar. Then she stood up, pulled a torch from her bag and shone it around the quarry and up the path.

"I'm alone. No threat, me. Especially not to a lady of the Craft." Sally sat and grinned at the old boy.

"Never disrespect a witch. I like that idea. More people should adopt it."

"Many have, m'd – Sally. Just those who know what's what."

He twisted and carefully tipped a generous amount from the bottle over the boulder behind him, muttering something quietly. Then he turned back with a flourish.

"With the niceties done, let's get down to the serious stuff. Ditch your coven, Sally m'girl. They're only dragging you down."

Sally spilt her drink and swore. Then looked him straight in the eye.

"So you agree. Time for me to get real. Back to the checkout."

He laughed; a rich, rolling thing that warmed the space between them.

"Oh gods. Yes and no to that. Do whatever you feel in the apparent world, but do not give up the Craft."

The fire suddenly flared as the boulder he leant against opened a great, emerald green eye. A voice sounded in her mind.

What the old windbag means is that you have potential. Your coven mates do not.

Sally tried to stand, fell backwards, tried to scream but the breath had been knocked from her. She lay there, mouth working, no noise coming out. The old man looked torn between embarrassment and laughter.

"Sally, this is Ettrin of the Rock."

He stood and rounded on Ettrin: "For pity's sake, dragon. I was warming up to introducing you."

When? Next century? Remember the last one you 'warmed up'? She tried to have you committed as a lunatic.

The old man waved his arms in frustration: "Of all the earthbound dragons I had to disturb, it had to be the one without manners!"

Manners? They would be what you used when you rained frogs on the Bishop of Lewes for waking you after a night cavorting with the Chanctonbury covens?

"That's completely different. The man had no respect for warlocks, witches or lie-ins."

She's laughing at us.

Sally tried to choke back the giggles, but the knowing tone in Ettrin's voice betrayed years of familiarity and companionship. She gave up and burst out laughing. The old man looked hurt.

Gradually the portent of the scene calmed her. She walked cautiously forward, peering at the eye. She looked askance at the old man.

"Who are you?"

"Just an old warlock, my dear."

His name is Matthew.

Ettrin raised an enormous eye ridge

And he's been hanging out in quarries for far too long.

Matthew looked at Ettrin.

"Subtle. Truly."

Sally looked back and forth.

"Aside from being astonished at not being hysterical, I'm curious. How did you get to be a rock, or is that in a rock, and how do you rain frogs on people?"

Sally smiled as she spoke. She could think of several candidates. Ettrin closed his eye then opened it again. A great weariness wound through the voice in her mind.

Dragons rarely slept to rest. Most of the time, they slept to pass the time. With the coming of man and the ebbing of the magic, they slept more to conserve their energies, apart from the few lucky enough to have lairs on ley lines. I chose to skip this age of supposed reason in sleep, merging myself with the earth. Many decades I slept, woken occasionally by those brave or stupid enough to crawl through the narrow caves and tunnels to my lair. Then came the Victorians, and their fascination with all things occult. A fascination with a Sussex legend of the cavern that contained a great oracle. Naturally, they used explosives to speed their work. If Matthew hadn't bought the land and had them thrown off it, I would have had to move, which could well have killed me. Heavily bonded to the

earth after so long asleep, the act of movement would have caused a
local earthquake and used so much of what little power I had that I
would have joined the rocks permanently.

Matthew smiled as he took up the tale.

"Much as I have in my time claimed to be Merlin, and Taliesin, or both, or
the same, I am actually a Victorian charlatan turned real warlock by a
chance meeting on the banks of the Thames. A wandering violinist stopped
me and gave me what I hope to have given you. The rhythm of the fall, a
beat that slows through the winter but speeds with the spring, making
changes all the time. I became far more than I had pretended to be, and
when my sight showed me Ettrin, I acted. Since then we have kept each
other company."

Ettrin turned his gaze to Sally.

Work your magic in this place, bring those of like soul when you
find them, or they find you. In quiet times, libate the rock and call
me up. The residue of your works will keep me. Just like it does
across the world. Covens and solitaires work the craft properly, in a
balance of gift and get, and the land is slowly restored.

*

There was an old quarry, now a nature reserve. The woman who manages
it had her companion buried there last year, next to the big boulder at the far
end. Some nights, the countryside ranger sees her sitting down there. Looks
like she's talking to his grave.

***

WINTER SONG

~ The Wheel of the Year; Transforming ~

*A tale from the today of 'These Pagan Isles' - a Britain
not quite as mundane as some would have us believe.*

Jamie left the noises of the party behind as he stepped out of the hall into the chill of the night. He took a deep breath to clear his head, then rubbed his face vigorously with his hands before looking about. More snow had fallen, its gentle sweep softening the shapes in the car park, making fantasy art of the playground and forming sparkling swathes in the moonlight that struck through the clearing clouds.

Far away, down toward the town, the amber of the streetlights struck contrast to the moonlit building tops. As the clouds cleared and the wind dropped, the quiet took on a life of its own, enfolding all but the party going on behind. Jamie looked back and smiled. Stephanie wouldn't miss him. It was her big night and big brother would only make her feel that she should behave herself. Jamie walked out of the car park and turned towards the town. A nightclub perhaps, or maybe a film. He'd still be back in time for the send off.

As he strode carefully on the quiet became more intense, and he marvelled at the absence of people about. Not a car, not a siren. An unusual Saturday night. Jamie walked on entranced by the silence and the glow of the snow in the moonlight.

As he walked past a snow laden bush, he dislodged a tumble of powdery snow that fell into a patch of moonlight spilling through a gap in the hedge. It lay there, an untidy pile of miniature jewels, glinting like a king's ransom in the silver light. Jamie crouched, reaching a finger to stir the pile. He remembered what his father had said about snow, many years before: "Its grand stuff, lad, and the fey love it, they do. For the winter months, they wear it as jewellery, and use it as goodwill coin."

A much younger Jamie had asked, "But when will I see the fey, father?"

His father had smiled and put a hand on Jamie's shoulder: "When you stop trying, Jamie lad."

"But if I don't look, I won't see 'em."

"I didn't say don't *look*, I said stop trying. Relax and they'll appear if you're worthy."

"Worthy? How do I get that?"

"Just be good, lad, be good. And not just do as you're told good either. Good is an all the time thing, not just when you're being watched. The fey are powers, laddie. If you're lucky you'll see some of the little folk, the Thanna Sidhe. But you'll have to be something special to see the Sidhe themselves."

"I'm going to see the Sidhe one day."

"That's as good a dream as I can think of, Jamie. Remember it."

Jamie had. Even after father had died and mother had dragged the family back to the city, Jamie had been the good one, always sacrificing his wishes to the needs of his family. After all these years, the dream of the Sidhe was something that made him smile, even though 'doing the good' had become second nature to him.

Reaching the outskirts of the town, Jamie paused and leant on a lamp post, looking about. A really beautiful night, he decided. As he looked back the way he had come, he saw a figure in a pale dress walking down the road toward him. For a moment he thought it was Stephanie, come to tell him off with a wicked smile before hooking her arm through his and leading him back to the reception. But the figure's pale gown was of plainer cut and as she approached, her gait betrayed her age. A little late for walking, Jamie mused before recalling with a grin that it was exactly what he was doing. As she came nearer it occurred to Jamie that her gown was also a little on the thin side for a freezingly clear night. Without a thought, he shed his jacket, stuffed his wallet into his trouser pocket and stepped forward to offer the protection of its warmth.

The woman stepped into the light of the moon, or the moon shone its light on her, Jamie was never sure which. He stopped, struck by a feeling of dread and correctness.

She stood almost regally, her grey hair turned silver by the moonlight hanging loose to her waist. She was slim and in the lines of her face could be seen the stunning beauty she must once have been. She regarded Jamie with eyes of icy blue lit with an implacable will. But she smiled and Jamie was smitten. This lady would have had men fighting over her in her youth.

"I'll not be needing your jacket, young man, but I am minded to be accompanied this night. The wheel turns and a meeting is ordained. Walk with me, scion of my consorts."

Jamie fell into step with the entrancing old lady, who still moved with a prescient grace made only a little more deliberate with age.

"It's a cold night to be out, madam. Could I ask where you are going? I could call you a cab on my mobile. Don't worry about the cost. A Christmas present from a stranger, shall we say?"

She stopped and her face lit with a smile. "You offer a gift to me? Do you know what you do?"

"Hmm, yeah. I'm going to call a taxi for an old lady out walking, so that she can get to her destination before she freezes. Or am I mistaken?"

Jamie's gentle sarcasm was accompanied by a disarming smile. It vanished as a cloak of silver thread appeared about the woman's shoulders.

"I am the winter queen and my mantle is cold, dark and still, son of man. But deep underneath, the fires of life still warm me. Under the cold, life still stirs."

Her voice was quiet, but with a ring of power that took Jamie to his knees. He stuttered in shock and awe. The woman cocked her head to one side and the smile returned.

"Come with me, oh man who would give his coat to the oldest lady."

With that, she turned and carried on walking down the street. Jamie struggled to his feet, and ran a little to catch up with her.

"I can't help feeling that I've stumbled out of my depth." he ventured.

She looked askance at him, the enigmatic smile still playing around her lips: "Way out. If not for my support, you'd drown."

"Thank you?"

With that, they walked on in silence. Jamie struggling to get a grip on the situation, the lady with an unstated intent.

She stopped, looking down an alleyway. With a swift nod she strode down it until she came to a moonlit doorway. In it lay a huddled form, a figure dressed in rags under a pile of dirty newspapers. She knelt by the sleeping but still shivering form. With a wave of her left hand frost shrouded the body, while with her right she gently plucked the azure flame that appeared at its brow. With a gentle smile she whispered to the flame before tossing it high, to be lost amongst the myriad stars.

Jamie stood, fear rising. Had he seen that? This old woman in a cloak of woven silver had just iced a tramp. Literally. He took a step back but stopped as she turned to face him. Her face wrinkled in consternation then cleared as she stepped swiftly forward. Too quick to stop, she touched her right hand to Jamie's brow. Jamie flinched but her left hand held his chin in a grip that brooked no avoidance.

"A gift for a gift, that is the way of it. Look with my eyes, son of man..."

Jamie looked, and tears started down his face as the breath caught in his chest.

All the buildings had become ghostly shapes, dull grey against a sky of the darkest blue, filled with stars that sparkled with all the colours of the spectrum. In the shadowy blocks little flames danced, flickered, flared or burnt low. Between the buildings flitted svelte forms on gossamer wings, decked only in jewellery made of snow crystals. They hunted new patterns in the icy flakes, and danced with delight when a new one was found. Jamie heard his father's voice, as if he were by his side again: "Thanna Sidhe, my boy. Oh, Blessed Be, Jamie."

Jamie looked, but his father wasn't there. He looked back at the lady, a thousand questions forming in his eyes.

She raised a finger and placed it on his lips: "No questions, scion of winter. This is a gift given freely, and questions do not go with gifts."

With that, she leant back against a fire escape and regarded Jamie through lowered brows. Then she looked up, where a sudden flare of fire lit the high skies. She smiled again.

"Dragons. Always showing off to the moon. Worse than wolves."

Jamie stood, dumbfounded. She turned back to him.

"My kindred and I are reckoned divine, but even we have our myths. A tale is told, on the rare occasions we meet, of the first gift: It is said that every soul flame has a candle, and all those candles burn in a great cavern of night."

She looked up at the stars.

"Every soul has its star, and every star its soul."

She smiled briefly, before looking back again.

"Most of the candles are blue. Some are white. Few are black. No one tends the candles now, but long ago, there was one. He was Consordat then, before he lost his son, his name and his power to intervene. Before he became the lonely god, it is said that he would often stand in that great cave, tending the candles, his calm restored by the lives he touched. But on the last time he visited that great fane, he found another there. A being from beyond crouched within, pouring wax from the black candles onto all of the white, so that every hero would be flawed. Consordat took his full mantle upon him and challenged the being. It laughed, and they both departed, forever opposed. But as the light from their mantles faded, another lit the walls, as a second being from beyond walked the winding paths. This being poured white wax upon all the blue candles, so that every soul has the potential to be a hero. Ptyrth is that being's name, and her mantle is balance. She watches the spiral dance still, her wings in the coming of night, her breath the shiver in the wind. And Mak Naur rages, unable to defeat her master stroke. That was the first gift. The spiral turns, cradle to grave, spirit to form and back again, and again. The gift is your free will, to find the hero within. It is a gift my kin cannot define or forfend. Treasure her gift, candle bearer; it will bring your kind to us one day."

Jamie stood in a cold alley, his jacket moving gently in the breeze that had sprung up. In a doorway nearby a body succumbed to rigor. The woman was gone and he was cold. Shaking his head like a man waking from a deep sleep, Jamie turned and hurried back to the reception.

As he approached the hall, he stopped and looked up at the nearly full moon, then down at the glistening snow around. He whispered to the night, "Oh father, you were right. Now I'll be as alone as you always seemed to be at times."

He turned toward the hall again, shoulders huddling against the cold. Then he stopped, the cold forgotten. He felt little hands lift a frozen tear from his cheek, and saw his exhaled breath swirl as unseen dancers whipped by.

A gentle voice, like the woman's, but softer, younger, whispered: "You have seen. You know. Never alone, scion of winter, never again."

***

THE HUNTER

~ Predator wings stroke the grey before dawn,
bearing a bright soul dark forlorn. ~

A tale from the realm of Khyr, drawn from
the early history of that mythical land.

My first story. This journey started by an Eisteddfod
fire many years ago, when people heard me tell this.

Talan prayed that it would be a bright, clear day as he slipped over the wooded ridgeline in the ghostly twilight before dawn. He moved confidently down to the left toward his vantage point, a weathered outcrop of moss-seamed rock partially obscured by a bramble thicket.

Tunnelling his way to his usual niche, collecting another batch of the tears and scratches that made his mother despair, Talan dared a peep over the rock into the shadowed valley below. Her lair was a darker patch at the foot of the cliff opposite, while only the occasional glint betrayed the presence of a pool under the great willow to the left of the cavern entrance. The old oak stood at the south end of the valley, its mighty spread concealing a large tract of scrubby ground in a shadow that would remain for some hours yet. The stillness of the pre-dawn lay unsullied by creature rustle or leaf murmur: she liked her mornings quiet.

Talan settled himself belly down, chin resting on the heels of his palms, watching for scavenger movements within her boneyard that lay to the right of the cavern entrance.

In the lulling silence, he remembered his first sally into the vale. It had been during a game of Thorn Tag, when he had disturbed a slumbering Tykynos while trying to evade the Malgun brothers. The beast had pursued the brothers, while Talan's panicked flight had ended when he had raced over the ridge top and plummeted down onto the very rock he now lay upon. Recovering from that impact he had glanced about, utterly lost. Down in the valley his gaze had fallen upon her for the first time, lying beside her pool. A metallic silver-grey mass the size of six carts, with talons the size of scythe blades upon gnarled feet that ended massive limbs. On the nearest of them her great head had lay, ridged with curving spines that were connected by translucent membranes. At that very moment, her head had lifted in a cavernous yawn, revealing a set of teeth the size of pickaxe handles, while a red forked tongue flicked negligently forth with the sound of a giant whip crack. The shock of seeing a dragon made Talan faint.

Talan did not return to the vale until he had recovered from the hiding his father had given him when he finally reached home. He had still been limping and pale when he was dragged to the Malgun boys' funerals, where the shockingly small caskets containing what the Tykynos had left were sent to the heavens on a pyre of yew and blackthorn.

About a moon passed after the funerals before his parents relented a little and Talan started slipping away to the valley as often as he could. Being the youngest son of an innkeeper meant a seemingly ceaseless series of dull, dirty, menial chores for which he was apparently supposed to be grateful. He was not. He did the minimum amount of work necessary to avoid a thrashing, and then only if a member of his family was nearby to ensure he did not escape. Given the slightest opportunity, he was off to his niche in the valley. He eluded all attempts to follow him and silently endured many painful questionings about his whereabouts during his absences. After a few months and many abortive efforts to confine or discipline him, his parents resigned themselves to his frequent day-long disappearances. They wrote it off as a phase he was going through.

By listening at the window looking out into the alley between the tavern and the bakery, shivering in the night air, or from beneath the pile of musty winter furs under the stairs in the taproom, Talan had discovered many things, a number of which he was sure his mother and elder sister would blush about. But he also found out that the dragon in the vale was known to men as Silversteel, a female of many years and great renown. She was also to be avoided at all costs. The travellers' tales said that she had slain and eaten two dozen knights of the realms, horses and armour included. Her valley was strictly off-limits to all children, but Talan was nearly a man so that didn't count.

He spent many a cheerfully petrified hour watching her roam the valley, calling forth the creatures of the woods by the power of her will. She would settle her body quietly to the ground before staring intently at a patch of growth. Within a few minutes, a glassy-eyed creature would stumble forth, making plaintive noises swiftly stilled by a blink of her silver eyelids. The denizen of the woods would then chitter or chirp or bark in a strange, communicative way before suddenly looking about in terror and plunging back into the verdure. Her reasons for this totally eluded Talan, but they must have been important, for she would often spend an entire day interrogating a succession of ensorcelled woodland creatures.

From his observations, Talan had concluded that the tales about ravening dragons were woefully exaggerated, as Silversteel only seemed to eat about once a week. This was a sickening but addictive sight, as the mighty beast glided effortlessly into the valley, carrying her prey in her front claws. She then reduced the captured oxen, sheep, Tykynos or horse to steaming wreckage with delicate but devastating claw swipes, before consuming the entire repast in four mouthfuls and a slurp or two.

But Talan's favourite pastime was watching Silversteel fly. She was graceful on the ground, but it was a calculated grace, the grace of something powerful holding itself in careful restraint. When she was airborne, there was no such restraint. She made tears of joy and wonder stream down Talan's face. Her flight always seemed to be accompanied by the distant strains of a complex melody, a tune one strains to hear but never quite catches. She flew for pleasure, it was obvious from the relaxed loops and rolls, the cloud-piercing ascents and flame-spewing dives, which terminated inches from the ground, gusting pale smoke across the valley as she soared upward again, wings outstretched, toward the sun. She rarely flew for more than a morning or an afternoon, probably because such aerobatics were a tremendous strain for one so huge. She would frequently settle and doze for a while afterwards, before leaping into the air again; the purpose in her movements revealing that she was off on the hunt.

Her speed was so exhilarating, her manoeuvres so graceful that Talan longed to leap into the valley, pleading for a ride, begging to be ecstatically terrified like no man in living memory. But he restrained himself with memories of the blood-curdling tales told about what dragons did to those who spied upon them, recounted in the late nights by slur-voiced drinkers at the inn.

One day several months ago Talan had seen another dragon in the valley, a small grey one that had been badly wounded in some unimaginable event. Talan found it difficult to conceive of anything that could injure a dragon, let alone kill one. The small dragon had talked with Silversteel for the entire day, in the spine-tingling and hackle raising tongue of the dragons, a language that many believed to be a myth. As they spoke Silversteel stared intently at the wounds upon the other, and Talan watched in awe as a nimbus of golden fire crackled about the wounds as they closed. This amazing feat seemed to be accompanied by another faint melody, more restrained, simpler than the flying tune.

When the sun had started to set the small dragon had departed at a speed that even Silversteel could not match. After that visit, Silversteel had lain virtually unmoving outside her cave for nearly a week before winging slowly away to hunt.

Then there had been the day when a knight had arrived at the inn, demanding directions to Silversteel's valley from Talan's father in a haughty voice. Talan had bribed his next oldest sister with his entire week's sweetmeat portion to take over his dishwashing so he could run to the valley.

Breathless he arrived to find that Silversteel was away, probably hunting. He carefully concealed himself in his niche, pulling brambles close and smearing dirt on his face, for it was said that the knights of the realms had formidable powers of observation. After a while the rhythmic sound of hoof beats betrayed the knight's approach, the mid-morning sun reflecting painfully bright from his sturdy metal armour, his lance pennon snapping lazily in the mild breeze. He had reined in his steed opposite the cave entrance, nearly in the thicket below Talan's rock. He had paused and then brought a twisted metal horn to his lips and blown himself a commendable fanfare before standing up in his stirrups to bellow his challenge: "Silversteel, foul creature of the ancients, I have travelled a hundred leagues to be your nemesis. Come forth and do battle, craven reptile!"

Due to the fact Silversteel was gone; the classic challenge received no reply. The knight waited a while before rising again and repeating his challenge. When that produced no dragon to fight, he slowly dismounted and cautiously reconnoitred the area. He had returned cursing after tripping over something in her bone yard and sprawling spectacularly in the semi-liquid mulch, covering his gleaming armour in lumps and streaks of rotted carrion and dragon droppings. He had to wash himself three times in her pool and polish his armour twice before he was satisfied with his appearance. His horse cropped grass, indifferent to the litany of profanities that accompanied his master's labours. Suddenly Silversteel glided into the valley from the north, arcing gracefully over the frantically mounting knight and making his horse shiver violently. Talan heard its barding rattle and the soothing murmur from the knight in the silence that descended as Silversteel landed.

The knight finished calming his steed and rose again to issue his challenge, changing "come forth and" in favour of the more appropriate "prepare to". The answer was swift and unexpected: "No."

The knight was obviously dumbfounded. He crashed down into his saddle, shaking his head. Talan gasped in wonder. She could speak the language of man!

The knight gathered himself.

"As I said, thou art craven!" he shouted, waving a mailed fist at her, while she casually threw an ox and two sheep into the cave mouth.

She slowly turned and levelled her gaze at the horse and rider. "I am not craven, o man. Nor am I deaf. I am merely attempting to reduce the wastage of capable knights."

"You impugn my ability, foul lizard!"

"I thought you would take it that way. Well, do you want to charge me or shall I just flame you and your nag down where you stand?"

The knight was clearly unhappy with the situation and the demeanour of his foe. He turned and rode toward the great oak, muttering imprecations to the heavens. There, he put on his great helm, settled his shield upon his arm and couched his lance into the ready position. Uttering a deep sigh and a single muttered word in the draconic tongue, Silversteel turned to face him. With a mighty wordless cry, the knight brought his lance parallel with the ground as he kicked his heels into his horse's flanks and commenced his charge. Talan held his breath as Silversteel slowly lifted her forequarters from the ground, exposing her scaled breast to the swiftly approaching, wickedly pointed tip of the lance.

The impact was tremendous, the knight grunting in surprise and lurching forward and up over his horse's head as it impaled itself upon Silversteel's poised tail and coming to a sudden, wetly screaming stop. That particular noise haunted Talan's nightmares for many years after. The knight himself described a graceful arc in the air, foreshortened as the tip of his lance dug into the ground, causing the weapon to bend and then splinter. With the support for his flight gone, the knight crashed down with a force that made Talan wince.

The armoured man climbed shakily to his feet as his horse vomited blood and slumped to the ground. He drew his sword. It was a strange weapon, with jagged saw-toothed edges instead of the fine, straight edges Talan associated with a knight's broadsword. He had cried a wordless denial at the sight of Silversteel withdrawing her gore-slicked tail from the limp body of his horse, held still by her right rear claw on its ribcage. She looked down and back at him over the still form, her voice sorrowful.

"It can end here, warrior. That blessed hacking blade you carry is not worth any of what the zealot who sold it to you claimed. It cannot harm me. Let it be, sir knight. Go home to your lord in honourable defeat."

The knight squared his shoulders and raised his sword in salute to his steed's body, then to his opponent.

"I hight Clomas Caer Morg, knighted son of Caer Morg. You have slain my faithful Blackmane, and you must now kill me."

He ran forward, sword raised. Silversteel swivelled to face him as he swung a mighty blow at her rump, which rebounded with a dull clang. She snapped out her right wing, hitting the knight across the abdomen and throwing him across the width of the valley, to land with a metallic thud and an agonised groan. She completed her turn in a more leisurely manner, furling her wings close against her back. Clomas regained his feet, retrieved his sword and advanced warily, sword weaving. With his free hand, he made a pass in the air, describing a triangular symbol, whilst muttering in a guttural tongue the likes of which Talan had never heard before. Silversteel must have recognised it because she suddenly reared up, spread her wings and spewed forth a gout of searing flame. Clomas leapt to his left, cursing loudly as his arcane working sputtered and died. Landing lightly, he seemed to recover quickly and charged toward the exposed underside of the dragon. Talan held his breath, but just as the knight completed his backswing, Silversteel dropped to her belly, wings furled and front legs lifted to allow her underside to impact the ground without mitigation.

The concussion shook the valley as a muffled scream died suddenly and bright, bright blood sprayed from under her as something gave way with awful snapping and grinding noises.

Talan had retreated, white-faced and with a hand clamped over his mouth. He paused several times on the way home to be violently and then just wrenchingly sick. He had avoided the valley for a whole week. But when he dared to return, there was no trace of Clomas Caer Morg, his horse or the battle.

A month ago, Silversteel had flown off early one morning with an indefinable air of intent about her. A few days later Talan had overheard a merchant telling a rapt audience a tale he had got from a courier riding for aid. The dragon Silversteel had descended on the duchies of the coast, extorting tithe in treasures and magic or laying waste to those unforthcoming. He had waited about ten minutes before letting his long-held dream take him to the valley. He had carefully watched and listened for a while, but reassured by the normal forest sounds so obviously absent when Silversteel was in residence, he clambered down into the valley and ran swiftly to the cave entrance.

Stepping inside, he pulled out a tallow candle and lit it with his father's 'lost' tinderbox. With a comforting wan light for company, he set off deeper into Silversteel's lair. It was a huge tunnel, many cart lengths long, with deep scoring upon the walls and floor. The air was heavy with a pungent musk that made Talan sneeze frequently until he adjusted to the thickly scented air.

After walking for what seemed like ages, he rounded a corner to be dazzled by the reflections that his little flame drew from the glittering horde before him. Coins and gems, jewellery and ornaments, weapons and armour: it all lay in a single immense pile with the occasional elegantly tooled cover of a great book or the wrought edge of a treasure chest protruding from the profusion of wealth. Talan's wonder and amazement faltered a little as he saw a row of battered shields hung on the wall behind the heap. Each one had a different heraldic blazon. He counted them, knowing the number before he began. Twenty five. The knights that had challenged her, their family or clan arms displayed like trophy heads around a lord's hall. The rightmost was sickeningly familiar, a black tower and grey wolf sanguine on a field of green, the arms of Caer Morg. Then Talan paused, surprised at the thought that drifted into his mind. At least the knights had come by choice to meet their doom, armed and ready. Each had died fighting. A hunted game animal would never have been accorded that privilege. Talan shook the sombre mood off and spent a delighted period of time rooting through and roaming over the precious nest, for that was what he discerned it to be. On top of all the treasures, a thick pad of uncountable large hides from more creatures than he had ever seen had been built up and pressed by Silversteel's tremendous weight into a solid bed.

Closer examination revealed that the bed rested on a low hummock of stone, which the treasure horde had been piled about. As he left the cave Talan attempted to consciously commit as much of what he had seen to memory as possible. He doubted he would have the opportunity or courage to take this chance again. That day remained the most precious of all his cherished memories.

A nebulous uneasiness pulled Talan from his remembering and he wriggled forward to watch Silversteel emerge from her cave, probably to spend the morning basking in the sun on the hard-packed earth outside. She would move cautiously forth, looking about the valley with her pupilless sapphire-blue eyes. Then after a moment her bulk would gracefully settle, haunches first, onto the earth. Talan had lain for hours, just watching the myriad colours that the rays of the sun reflected from her scales as her immense lungs stirred the scaled hide. Talan peered down, eyes narrowing as they adjusted to the light before going wide with shock.

The impossible had happened!

Silversteel lay like a broken doll across her sunning place, her flawless hide rent and smashed. Her angular head was a darkly convoluted mass from the base of her upper jaw back to her batwing shaped ears. Gazing in fascinated horror, he saw that the willow was but a smoking stump, while her pool lay scattered across the gouged and pitted valley floor in the form of murky puddles. Several swathes of barren, blackened ground mutely attested to the savagery of the battle. He stood up on the rock to get a better view of the devastation, before scrambling down to the valley floor. Just as he took a step toward her cave, a pair of baleful yellow eyes opened in the shadows under the great oak. The voice that accompanied that event was deep and rasping.

"Stand still, manling."

Talan froze.

"Now come hither, I shall not harm thee."

Talan's reluctant approach faltered as he made out the sheer, staggering size of the deeper dark within the shadow of the oak.

"Keep coming. My shadow cannot crush thee, nor can my breath burn thee."

Faintly reassured, Talan moved to about a cart's length from the edge of the shade of the mighty tree. As the first rays of sunlight illuminated the cliff above Silversteel's lair, the eyes blinked as reflected light brought definition to its form. Talan gasped and paled. Another dragon! But this one blacker than night and at least twice as large as Silversteel.

"Tell me, manling. What do you see?"

Talan swallowed and after two stuttering starts, managed to reply: "A dragon, my lord."

"Good."

A smile showed yellowed teeth taller than Talan, and he sat quickly before his legs failed him completely. He breathed deeply, head spinning.

"You are not entirely incoherent in my presence, then. A refreshing change."

A deep chuckle bent the grass, raised gooseflesh on Talan's arms and briefly choked him in the miasma of blood and carrion. He gathered himself, youthful curiosity overriding his fear.

"What's in-co-here-ent, lord?"

"Unable to speak, little manling. Which you are not. I am pleased."

"Does that mean you're not going to eat me?"

Despite every effort, the query emerged as a breathy squeak. The great fanged smile appeared again.

"I was not going to eat you anyway. I was going to tell you a tale."

The answer was so unexpected, Talan just stared.

"Did you know she watched you, up there, under the brambles?"

"She did?"

Another squeak. Talan flicked a wary glance over his shoulder and swiftly wished he had not. Silversteel's head was a nauseating mess, clearly revealed in the morning light. He swallowed hard and turned his attention back to the shadowed monster.

"Oh yes. She said I could tell you our story so that one day mankind will know the truth."

"But what if I forget? And how can I let all the people know when I can't even write my own name?" Talan's voice wailed into the sudden absolute silence.

"You *will* remember." A simple statement, the emphasis cracking like thunder. Talan felt something slide within his mind.

"Now listen well, young -?" The eyes flickered in question.

"Talan Donal Berris, lord."

"Now listen well and hear my saga, Talan Donal Berris. I am named Salaxon, called Darkforge many centuries ago, now known only as Bane." Talan's incredulous delight at being given a dragon's true name turned to grim horror as the final name registered with his scant teaching. Bane, a dragon that slew dragons, hunter over all the earth for twenty centuries, a feared nocturnal visitor that left the great beasts dead, their gem hard eyes unseeing the dawn that brought the curious, the greedy and the bigoted to gloat over their passing.

"I see you know me, Talan. Now know my history. In life I flew with the King's Wing, thirty of the greatest dragons to ever take fire under the Mother Sun. We fought many wars to make the land habitable for the coming folk, the humanoid races. The final war was the greatest and the most infamous. We rallied with King Flinaessa and his mages to rid the world of Mezlorahn."

Again Talan's scanty learning reared its shaggy head and spat grim details
from memory to consciousness; Mezlorahn, called the Mad, a mage of such
evil that his name alone was said to be able to conjure up demons. Ruler of
the bloodiest empire ever known on Khyr, defeated in the battle that saw his
evil citadel destroyed. Bane's smoky cough brought Talan swiftly out of his
contemplations.

"I will not bore you with the details of the campaign we fought against his
draconian demons and their minions, but bring you to that final battle that
raged along Chacsom Gap, a sheer-sided canyon that ended in a massive
granite overhang, under which lay the blood stained gates of Caer Mordis,
Mezlorahn's ancient stronghold. We, the King's Wing, had been reduced to
seventeen by the intense fighting of that summer, but those that remained
were fearsome and beautiful. I was the youngest, having only three
thousand seasons upon me. Asarth and Kirlus, the oldest males, led the first
wave into that canyon. They perished, but the second wave, led by Koro and
Shuenna, my parents, breached the gates and stormed through. The great
courtyard that lay beyond became the resting ground of all but two of the
King's Wing. It also marked the end of Mezlorahn's demon dragons and all
his remaining forces. We fought from dusk to dusk to stand before the doors
of his sanctum. The bodies and debris lay chest deep in blood and ichor, for
in the battle many of you little folk were crushed or batted aside. The very
air itself was deadly from the breath and magics of so many dragons.
At the last, I and Silurana, my chosen, vied for the duty of entering the
dread hall where he waited, at bay but also at his most lethal. I cheated and
entered before she could realise my deception.

Within that dark place I fought as I have never done before or since.
Mezlorahn had six of the fallen host at his call, such was his power. I
dispatched two of the dark angels with words of power, invoked our

Mother's name to send three others screaming home to the abyssal plains. The final one, Strathang, one of the angels of war, I had to fight. It took me two hours and cost me my sight, my left wing and broke most of my ribs, but I rent him beyond even demonic aid. Strathang died laughing, which disturbed me. After healing myself with the last of my magics and charring Strathang's remains with a dribble of my fire, I moved through the devastated halls to find Mezlorahn in his damned library, surrounded by the mutterings of his evil tomes."

"But books can't speak, can they?"

Talan wasn't sure. Ever since the clergy had circulated the missive on 'The Dangers of Literacy to Faith', every book, scroll and parchment in Talan's village had been reduced to ashes.

"Evil works take on a life of their own after a time, to aid in suborning those that use them to the dark power's influence. Mezlorahn was so evil that the tomes actually flocked to him, by means that left many a potential dark wizard and hundreds of innocents insane, soulless or worse. His library was the greatest and most blasphemous collection of literature and arcane lore ever assembled."

Bane paused, shifting his wings with the sound of stone sliding on ashes.

"Oh, his tomes cackled and whispered as I widened the doorway to enter. He drew himself up, reviling the dragon kin, speaking condescendingly of our abilities and magics, for no spell could touch his earthly form. He caressed his arcane staff as he spoke, madness in his eyes. I nearly succumbed to the emanations of that relic, but then he laughed and poured scorn on our Mother, deriding our love of flying in the Mother Sun's light. My rage at his arrogant mouthings broke the evil influence, but I waited, outwardly calm, as his tirade drew to a close."

Talan looked about, surprised that the sun had only risen a little way. He stretched his legs and then settled, turning his attention back to the great creature in front of him.

"Finally, he asked me in mock terror if I intended to rend him. I have cherished the look on his face as my flaming breath sloughed the flesh from his bones for all these long years. I had deliberately saved my incendiary venom because I knew that only dragonfire could truly injure a necromancer of his power. But in the long battle with the fallen ones and my healing thereafter, I had lost track of the time. It was night and the infernal powers that abetted Mezlorahn's might had awakened. The entire library erupted in vengeful fury even as my fiery breath destroyed it. Black flames of malevolence that blew the entire face of Caer Mordis out of Chacsom Gap into the camped armies. The carnage was terrible."

"But what happened to you and the lady dragon?"

"Silurana had departed, as her time of clutching was near. I died."

Bane's eyes glittered in the reflected sunlight.

Talan's eyes went wide. He paused, took a deep breath and then with a look of resigned fear, asked: "But if you died, what are you doing here?"

The undead had a nasty repute. Undead dragons he had never heard of, but they were probably horribly nastier in ways that only sages and priests would know. Bane's discomforting smile blossomed again.

"I died in that unholy blast, but I found no rest. Mezlorahn had invoked one of the great host, the one known as the 'Angel of Fates'. Its delight is laying curses upon things. As a child of the Mother Sun, I was a welcome victim and my curse was a joy to its black heart. I was reformed, whole but black as night, the only one of my kind to ever exist. From that moment forth, I had to consume dragons to survive. To die, I had to slay every dragon in Khyr. In this half life, I could only function by night and the smell of a dragon drove me into a feeding frenzy that overwhelmed any chance of restraint. Thus I was lost to the Mother Sun's light and from dragonkind. Over the years I came to accept my fate, leaving warnings at the scenes of my kills to reach my former kin."

Bane's voice had fallen to a rumbling whisper. Talan leapt to his feet in outrage.

"But why didn't you fight it?"

"At first I tried, but the hunger drove me on. To a dragon, survival is the greatest urge. It dominates all our actions. I would find myself in flight after settling to starve and die in a secluded area. I would black out and my hunger would lead me to the nearest dragon. When it came within range of my supernaturally heightened senses, the feeding frenzy would drive me to kill."

"Didn't they try and stop you?"

"Oh yes, many times. But the nature of my unlife is resilient. I have but one way to die, and until that condition is fulfilled, I cannot die. I can be driven off by severe injury, even apparent death. But I recover. The longest it has taken me is an entire cycle of the moon, and that was after I had been blasted to dust by a group of mages who then summoned a ghostwind to scatter my motes all over the world. Besides that, dying gives me blinding headaches for weeks afterwards."

"Couldn't they just keep killing you?"

"You do not realise just how much it takes to really hurt me, let alone seriously injure me. That group of mages had been preparing for two years and I had given them my true name to enhance the ritual's effectiveness."

"So you kill them when you find them. That's- Hey! The sun's up. How come you haven't blown up or something?"

Bane turned his head to the sky, then slowly returned his attention to Talan. His voice came as a whisper rich with emotions that Talan just couldn't grasp.

"Because I have finished, Talan Donal Berris. Silversteel was the last. There are no more dragons left in Khyr."

His sorrow was almost palpable.

"What about you?"

"I am dead. I am not a dragon. Dragons are magnificent creatures that fly beneath Mother's watching eye, living in symphony to man's plaintive song."

"But you're not dead. You're living. So where's the curse now?"

"On my last day, the angel said, I would see the Mother Sun rise, but she would take my tainted soul as she set. I have a day in her light as a reward for my cursed deeds of the last centuries, an irony not lost on that angel."

"So you're going to die at sundown?"

"Yes, Talan. I will be the last shadow of dragonkind to pass from this land."

Talan looked up, desolation in his gaze: "So there won't be any more dragons?"

"They will return eventually. Khyr will not be dragonless for long. I think they will be back before you grow too old, Talan. But I doubt any will clutch on Khyran soil for many centuries to come."

"So what do you do now?"

"I wait for sundown, my final sunset. I have longed for and dreaded this day."

"Why not fly? You said all dragons loved it."

"I could not, even if I dared. Silversteel tore my wings in the battle, but even if she had not, I would not stain the sky with my damned shade."

"Why Silversteel last? She's been here for ages and many knew of her."

"Because she was my daughter. She was the result of Silurana's clutching after that battle at Chacsom Gap, a beautiful silver dragonette that sought her cursed sire for two centuries before she confronted me at the scene of one of my kills."

"But why didn't you kill her then?"

"Another feature of my curse. I could not gorge myself. After I killed, I was left to the loathing that rose within me at my crime. It would plague me for days and drive me near insane with grief. So one night as I recovered from the frenzy of a kill, just before my grief took me, she came to me. She hovered there, all moonlit and crying her love and pity. We talked for most of the night and then she departed so she could be far away before my hunger rose again. Since that night, I have flown with a purpose. I have spent twenty centuries slaying every other dragon in Khyr so that she could live to a full wing. She has, even clutching twice, but outside Khyr's borders, so that her children will be safe from their grandsire's curse. That was my message to my kindred: I am cursed to kill, but I shall take those ready or willing to die first. They agreed to my plan, and so for many years I took dragons that came to me, whether out of compassion, ennui or age, I do not know and could not ask."

"What happened when you ran out of dragons that came to you?"

"Finally I had to start on the unwilling, but by then many eggs had been clutched outside the borders of Khyr. My curse stipulated every dragon hatched on Khyran soil. I have had to travel a long way to slay some of them, but in the end, I could not delay any longer. I fought my hunger for eight months so that my kill would be quick. She very nearly slowed me down, but my cursed unlife gives me the advantage of being able to ignore any injury that is not immediately debilitating or what would normally be fatal. Due to my age, size and power, I am formidable. But she fought her best regardless, my beautiful Silvastra."

Bane's voice had attained a husky quality that kept Talan swallowing lumps in his throat and brushing away tears.

In silent mockery of the tragedy below, the morning was beautiful and clear, a day to bring smiles to the menfolk and a lightness of step to the maids. In villages across the land, children plotted escape from chores whilst parents awaited the attempted breakouts with a loving resignation. A birdsong drifted, incongruously cheerful, into the silence of the valley. Talan finally summoned up the courage to ask: "Bane, what about Silversteel's treasure?"

"So it was you who saw it." A statement, backed with an unwavering stare.

"Well, she was out, and I didn't take anything, and I never told."

"Good thing for you. A dragon can sense if its horde has been disturbed or if anything is taken. It is a fool who steals from a dragon, and a fool who has only a short while to live, at that."

"But what now?"

"Let them have it, Talan. It is of no use to Silvastra now. But I am sure she would have wished you to pick a few things from it. She liked you."

Talan sat, speechless. Bane stretched his ragged wings, settling them back carefully, taking several minutes. Then his gaze turned fully on Talan.

"Would you stay with me today, Talan? There is nothing else that dares to stand vigil."

Talan stayed with the ancient, sad creature as the day passed by. Bane spoke quietly, reminiscing about his living days, taking Talan on vocal wings to far places and strange views, speaking of his youth in the snow-capped mountains to the west, of sojourns in the long sunken courts of Salass, amongst an aquatic elfin race long retreated from the knowledge of

III

man. Finally, as the sun began to descend he spoke of the dragon kindred, of flying in praise, the purity of the magic word and the gifts of fire. Talan sat rapt and entranced as he received history in its purest form; from one who had seen it happen and had no ability to lie. But as the sun dipped low behind Silversteel's lair, Bane fell silent and his scintillant eyes closed.

Talan waited, unsure what to do. Then Bane began to quietly hum, a low monotone that drifted into a crooning, mournful, wordless tune which seemed to fill the valley and call to things far away. As the last light left and the valley sank into twilight, Talan heard Bane's song interwoven with his last words.

"Mother, although I have slain my kindred, your children, bless me into darkness that I may rest at last."

From far above and further away, Talan heard a gentle voice calling.

"Salaxon, come home. Come to us, Darkforge."

From the black body shot a grey form that spread spectral wings as it ascended to the sky. Turning silver in the last light of the sun, his mournful song turned sweet at last, the spirit of Salaxon flew down the last rays into his Mother's embrace.

"Remember us, Talan Donal Berris." The gentle voice nought but a whisper, fading, gone.

As the evening star sparked into shine, so the dark body crumbled to dust. Wiping his tears away, Talan ventured into Silversteel's lair, careful not to look at her remains again. He moved slowly, using his touch on the wall until he heard his footsteps start to echo. Then he lit his precious candle. Searching the horde he took a small sword, a hand axe, some beautifully made leather boots and a suit of fine mail. Filling a pouch with coins and gems, he rested in the lair on Silversteel's great nest until the following dawn.

Striding into the shadow of the great oak, he turned and raised his new sword in salute to the still body outside the cave, and to the dusty outline in front of him. Wiping his eyes quickly, he sniffed hard and turned to head northeast, toward the big cities and places where he could learn to read and write.

***

THE FALL OF FLOWER DREAM

A tale from the past of the world of 'These Pagan Isles' – a place not quite as mundane as history would have us believe.

As this tale contains many Japanese words and concepts, there is a glossary at the end.

The katana cut the air in a simple cross cut, turned into art by the curve described between blows. Cherry blossoms parted cleanly as the four-man blade cut clean without tearing a petal, the setting sun flashing reflections from the mirror sheen of the unblemished blade and ornately wrought gold and lacquer tsuba.

Sososuke finished the movement in a full right lunge, left leg almost parallel to the ground, her right leg folded neatly under her body weight, giving a deceptive hint of vulnerability despite being easily able to lift her clean off the ground with a single, smooth push. Her right knee pointed toward Yoritomo and her eyes never left the point in the far distance where her budo focus lay.

Yoritomo applauded thrice, a great boon. He turned to his councillors.

"I am minded to grant this warrior her request. She is the very spirit of Moonsword manifest in a lesser form. She has striven to overcome that with a will that many of my purported masters of Bushido would do well to take lessons from."

His words caused a polite ripple of concern amongst the seated gathering. In truth, the shock was profound, but those who sat on the Minamoto clan council knew they were bound to maintain an air of imperturbability even if the Ineluctable Dragon of Fuyu-ho should deign to descend upon their illustrious gathering. Pan-cho, tutor to the lord's son, bowed himself to the tabletop without getting his whiskers wet in the bowl of sake under his nose, an art that baffled many present. Yoritomo snapped his fingers in acknowledgement.

"Honoured, while your generosity is renowned and we all revere your noble intent to promote any with merit, is this not a step too far?"

Yoritomo turned to face him. The council readied their fans to shield themselves from sudden sprays of blood should the master of Minamoto decide Pan-cho had overstepped.

"You are indeed correct, my learned councillor. It is precisely that. I am in a robust mood today and feel the need to challenge one of my glorious ancestor's more ludicrous rulings."

The silence went from profound to anticipatory as gazes shifted to Li-fan, Master of the Budoka and self-assured of being the greatest samurai currently incarnate. He seemed to be having difficulty forming words around the conflicting actions of screaming in fury and remaining utterly composed. Eventually his choler eased and he bowed to the tabletop, having moved his sake to one side.

"Respectfully, Honoured, I beg for you to reconsider. I dread the repercussions should this decision become general knowledge amongst the samurai in your service."

Yoritomo smiled while he watched the venerable warrior simmer awaiting his reply. Li-fan was overly enamoured of the authority bequeathed to him by his hereditary position, which gave him the power of life and death over the deadliest warriors to walk this land. In an obtuse interpretation of the Bushido code, it made Li-fan their *de facto* commander, a fact he was all too happy to remind people of. This time, he was going to be disappointed.

"My dear Li-fan. I agree. Thus, I shall not place such a desperate conflict upon you. I deem that Sososuke and her dojo shall fall under the auspices of my honourable cousin Yoshinaka."

Li-fan was caught. He had raised the objection couched in terms of his influence and insinuating that his disapproval could cause unrest. Ronin were bad for a lord's reputation. Yoritomo had obviously anticipated him. In so many ways he brought his father's talent for intrigue to new levels of irritation. Outmanoeuvred, Li-fan placed his hands flat on the table and touched his forehead to them.

"Your perspicacity is enhanced again, Honoured."

As Li-fan straightened up, the other councillors sat like breathing statues as they tallied the complex webs of obligation, favour and power in the light of this unexpected humbling of Li-fan. Yoritomo turned back to Sososuke. He clapped his hands once.

"Rise, Sensei of the Flower Dream. I trust your bushi will do you credit. Do you wish to have an inaugural tournament against Li-fan's elite? It is your right for his implied slight upon you."

Sososuke flicked her gaze briefly to Li-fan as she rose smoothly to a relaxed stance, not a movement betraying the agony in her legs from holding position while the discussion had concluded. Li-fan was holding rigidly still while his features tried to cover an expression better suited for one who had swallowed a hornet. She sheathed her katana and bowed to Yoritomo in one smooth movement. Iaido disciplines were never a wasted art as some proclaimed.

"Honoured, I am humbled by your generosity. Your offer is far more than the Flower Dream deserves. But as you know, the followers of Moonsword-Ryu never compete."

Yoritomo clapped his hands in glee and laughed out loud.

"You are marvellous! Indeed, the Celestial Mistress of your School does not approve of her art being used for show. Fighting is for survival. Depart us now and take news to your dojo. Yoshinaka will be with you by the new moon, by which time you will be ready to be recognised as the Flower Dream, budo school of the weaker gender under his patronage. Yoshinaka will have my seal to bestow the status of samurai upon you and yours if he deems you worthy."

The matter forgotten, Yoritomo spun back to his council to see Hamakai floating in a perfect lotus pose over the spot left vacant for him. He nodded to the venerable kisai as he extended his hand for one of the geisha to provide him with a drink. They would know from the place and the time of day what he wanted. Hamakai coughed politely and spoke without waiting for permission.

"I see a schism caused by your wayward plotting. Sososuke may be greater than any swordsman seen in this age, but she is not subject to the weaknesses of her sex and thus unpredictable in ways you cannot perceive."

Yoritomo sipped his tea.

"Venerable kisai, your advice is sage as usual. But in this, permit that my actions and understanding of the ramifications exceed your reservations?" Hamakai bowed, touching his forehead to his crossed ankles. He remained thus as he faded from view. Yoritomo smiled.

"We are adjourned. I shall bathe, then sign the missive to Yoshinaka that will be prepared with a messenger waiting by that time. Fair sakura time to you, worthies."

With that, he left at a brisk pace before any could consider bowing to interrupt his departure. Li-fan rose and stormed off, muttering. He cuffed his aides repeatedly as they tied his daisho on. It was duly noted that he was officially in a very bad mood and not to be disturbed until the following day.

*

Later that night, Li-fan put aside his public outrage and donned the uniform of a common bushi. Thus disguised he left his dwelling and journeyed through the city to an old bathhouse where one could find introductions to lesser kisai and spirit-talkers. After sharing a drink there and leaving far more chits than a mere drink required, he followed the whispered instructions to a deserted graveyard. At the edge of that place of ill-fortune an elegant caravan sat, its wheels long lost to the plants that twined them. He paused, took a deep breath and tapped thrice on the nearest wheel rim with the hilt of his tanto.

From within there was a slight movement and the door opened. A cloud of incense smoke lit from within by jade lanterns removed any chance of him having any warning of attack. As it was, a wordless greeting summoned his body within before he could react. With a crash, the door closed. He looked about frantically before the smoke vanished and he beheld Sifa, current mistress of the Waning Moon Court, a cadre of kami much taken with meddling in the affairs of men. She smiled a knowing smile.

"Geisha samurai. Who would have thought it of Yoritomo to bestow such honours upon his bed mates?"

Li-fan bristled, before calming himself by visible act of will. He had been warned that kami of this court delighted in baiting nobility.

"Indeed, lady. It is the heart of my concerns that the spirit of my warriors be broken by knowing that their worth has been sullied."

"Ah, you believe that this Flower Dream may resort to arts more suited to the bedroom than the battlefield when their sword arms and wills prove to be weak?"

"I am sure that this may have occurred during their rise to prominence. The dogs in the provinces would trade their mothers for a night of sport. They would consider kenjutsu training a bargain in exchange for the delights offered by these so-called warrior maidens. It would also make them tolerant of such an insult to their martial prowess."

Sifa nodded.

"I sense you have a plan, honourable Li-fan. Explain it to me."

Li-fan smiled. It was good to be recognised as one of leadership qualities.

"The virtue of the Flower Dream must be established. Then it must be watched in case it slip or be used for gain."

"Indeed."

"The problem is establishing the virtue of the retinue of Sososuke. They are wary of all outsiders. Such a request could be taken as dire insult."

Sifa smiled a knowing smile: "Ah, honoured Li-fan, the answer is simple. Near the dojo of the Flower Dream is a wine house. The maidens go there regularly like men would. While I know that to be disgraceful, it does offer the opportunity you need."

Li-fan looked disgusted and then puzzled: "I do not see how geisha disporting themselves as bushi can help me."

Sifa gazed over Li-fan's head: "I have access to that wine house as the owner owes me his son's life. So as opportunity arises, I shall arrange for two or three of them to be given tears from the white lotus in their sake. Then as the juice fuels their desires, I shall take them gently and thus see if they are unblemished."

She looked sharply at Li-fan: "You are welcome to send an observer to ensure that nothing is missed."

Li-fan seemed to give the matter serious consideration as a flush spread from his collar to his hairline. He nodded: "I would feel better not risking my men's honour in such scandalous endeavours. I could not ask them to do something that I was not prepared to do myself."

Sifa smiled a little smile before composing her features to show awe at his noble sacrifice: "I shall make arrangements. You will need to be able to free yourself from your duties at a day's notice and be absent without query for a day or two. This will be necessary on several occasions."

Li-fan nodded, his thoughts clearly elsewhere. With barely another word, he gave her a wad of chits without even looking at their value and departed swiftly. Sifa laughed. Aging men of nobility were so easy to lead.

*

At first, Yoshinaka was horrified at his cousin's command. He spent the day furiously taking his frustrations out on his sparring partners. Bad enough that his cousin's jealousy over his love for Tomoe, the daughter of a minor lord beholden to Minamoto, had driven that lord to send his daughter far away to continue her education. It had been that or spark an unseen battle that would have ruined him and left his daughter a geisha in Minamoto servitude.

But now he was placing Yoshinaka in charge of a tradition- and ancestor-insulting whim to have his own force of female samurai? The concept was so alien that he did not see the dangers until later.

After he finished bathing he dismissed his geisha, being in no mood for their carefully controlled performances of desire. He resolved to read for the evening. Relaxed and clad only in a robe, he entered his sanctum to be startled by the presence of a ninja-suited figure kneeling respectfully between the window and his desk. He took in the fact that the visitor had no weapons and then allowed curiosity to take him where it would while maintaining a good distance from the figure.

"You are skilled, warrior. I do not think that any have entered this far into Minamoto territory ever before."

"That is correct, lord. Fortunately I am a messenger, not an envoy of death."

The female voice startled him. He had heard rumours that the ninja clans trained women as well as men, but this was the first confirmation he had received.

The visitor raised her head and removed her night-kami mask. He recognised her face instantly.

"Sososuke."

Yoshinaka was astonished. She should be miles way, riding joyfully to her dojo with news of Yoritomo's decision.

"A double surprise, sensei Sososuke. I presume that you have some serious purpose. Do you bring a secret message from my cousin?"

She smiled and shook her head: "I bring you news of your cousin, but nothing from him. Please, seat yourself lord. I bear you no malice this night. Quite the opposite, in fact."

Yoshinaka seated himself. His damn curiosity was piqued into a near frenzy, but his outward calm was undisturbed. Taking a pipe from the table beside the chair, he gestured for Sososuke to continue as he tamped himself a much needed bowlful.

"You have been given my dojo to oversee. You alone hold the authority in your cousin's name to make us samurai, an unheard-of thing. As your cousin is head of the clan, you will abide by his wishes. Seeing that my dojo is not unfit and my maidens are all masterful, you will give your consent and Yoritomo will applaud your diligence."

Yoshinaka began to feel unease. She had summed up his next season's work and the inevitable result very well.

Sososuke continued: "You will suggest to him what battles and skirmishes we could be useful in. We will surprise all with our prowess. You will gain face despite our unusual nature. Things will seem to be going very well."

Sososuke paused as he lit his pipe.

"Sometime in the spring, it will be discovered that maidens of the Flower Dream are disporting with kami in a local wine house. Li-fan will be caught observing the improprieties and as his last act before committing seppuku, he will attest to the fact that all participants were doing so of their own free will. The outrage will focus attention on the Flower Dream. Then you will be revealed as having taken several of the maidens as your geisha in orgies of dishonour. Your fall will be total. Yoritomo will regretfully take your lands and then exile you if you do not commit seppuku first."

Yoshinaka sat, feeling the weight of shame as if it had happened already. Then his anger rose: "I would never dishonour a maiden warrior, no matter that I find the concept of such a woman utterly strange."

Sososuke nodded: "I understand. Your actions will be seemingly freely made, but in fact you will be driven by white lotus tears administered by kami from the Waning Moon Court. Their mistress, Sifa, is being paid a lot by your cousin to rid him of obstacles to uniting the Minamoto clan. He would have involved you, but his lust for Tomoe and jealousy of you has blinded him utterly to reason in this."

Yoshinaka sat and finished his pipe. He then cleaned it, tamped it full and smoked another bowl while his mind whirled. Finishing it, he pointed the stem of the pipe at Sososuke.

"I see what you say, but I cannot see your part in this. What could you gain from keeping this clan divided and your dojo unrecognised?"

She lifted herself on her fingertips, swinging her legs from a kneeling stance into a full lotus before placing herself down on the mat, with barely a whisper of sound from the whole manoeuvre. She looked at the ornate screen across the room as she spoke, her eyes distant.

"I am not meant to be here. I should have died at birth but the Lady of the Moon Court came into me with a purpose. I have lived a life shaped by the purest budo to start a change."

"What change?"

"The perception that women are just as capable as men. That the strength of partnership is far more than can ever be achieved by dominance. You and Tomoe will be proof of that."

Yoshinaka sat up as his eyes narrowed, his pipe dropping to the floor.

"That is the second time you have mentioned her. What do you know of Tomoe?"

Sososuke turned her face to him, her eyes losing their far-off stare.

"Tomoe is my cousin, lord. She loves you and needs you. Never have I seen such a passion as she carries for you. She is the finest of the Flower Dream except for me, and I am not entirely human."

Yoshinaka took several minutes to compose himself while his intrigue-schooled mind worked through the situation. Then he looked at her again.

"I suspect that to complete this little piece of yours, I am to deny the Flower Dream its contentious status, then rescue a lady of Minamoto from its inglorious withering, only to miraculously discover that we are suited and sue for marriage before next spring?"

Sososuke smiled again and snapped her fingers in approval.

"Very good, lord. The only omission would be for me to capture an agent of the Waning Moon Court about to administer poison to you. The niceties of what it was meant to do to you will be lost in the fact that he was trying to do it. From there the Moon Court will be able to justifiably intervene to limit the meddling of the Waning Moon Court in the affairs of man at last."

Yoshinaka stretched himself and chuckled: "I think I should rest now. I have to start a tiresome trek to some dojo full of women aspiring to be samurai tomorrow."

Sososuke covered her smile in her mask and bowed fully to him.

"Indeed, my lord. The fall of the Flower Dream will be lost to history as a shameful episode. But the concept of the onna bugeisha will find substance in Tomoe if you allow her to flourish fully as your wife and first captain."

He nodded: "I find the concept to sit well with me. Even allowing for my tendency to indulge Tomoe, I feel it is right."

He looked up, puzzlement on his face: "But '*Onna bugeisha*'?"

Sososuke spun on the ball of her left foot where she was poised on the window ledge: "A term for high caste women who will fight with their lords to protect their territories and families. They will provide confidence for their lords while they are on campaign in the knowing that their homes are defended."

Yoshinaka looked down as he refilled his pipe: "It is not a term I am familiar with."

From outside, a receding voice laughingly replied: "Lord Yoshinaka, we can hardly call them female samurai, now can we?"

***

THE FALL OF FLOWER DREAM: GLOSSARY

(Please note that any grammatical or technical misuse is wholly my fault.)

Budo	'Martial way'. The practice of combative arts to enhance spiritual enlightenment. An experiential path.
Budoka	A practitioner of the martial arts.
Bushi	Soldier
Bushido	A relatively modern term for the code of conduct of the samurai that arose between the 9th and 12th centuries.
Chit	A form of currency made from wooden tokens marked with varying values and usually carried on a cord.
Daisho	The pair of swords carried by the samurai, nowadays expected to be a katana and a wakizashi of matched fittings, but originally any combination of a long sword and another sword longer than a tanto.
Dojo	'A place of the way'. Any building where formal training in one of the many martial arts is conducted.
Four-man blade	In feudal Japan, swords were graded by how many criminals or peasants they could cut through in a single blow with the hapless victims laid on top of one another.
Fuyu-ho	Mount Fuji
Geisha	A woman trained in the arts of courtly entertainment, which may or may not include those of a sexual nature. Renowned for their subtlety, strength and grace.
Iaido	The art of drawing, striking, clearing and sheathing the katana in a few smooth movements. A meditational discipline bound by rigorous protocol due to its

	historical lethality when practiced freely.
Kami	Spirit or spirits.
Katana	The classic primary weapon of the samurai, a single-edged sword with a slight curve to the blade and a blade length of over 23 inches.
Kenjutsu	The art of swordsmanship.
Kisai	Wizard.
Ronin	A samurai without a lord to serve due to his master's death, his master's fall from favour or his own dismissal.
Ryu	A particular discipline or school of martial arts.
Samurai	The military noble class of pre-industrial Japan. Exclusive to men as women were considered inferior in all ways.
Sakura	Cherry blossom
Sensei	A respected and experienced teacher
Tanto	A single-edged dagger with a straight blade between 6 and 12 inches in length.
Tsuba	The guard at the end of the grip of bladed Japanese weapons. Contributes to the balance of the weapon as well as providing protection for the wielding hand/s.
Wakizashi	Short sword in the same style as the katana with a blade length between 12 and 23 inches.

This story occurs during the late Heian period of feudal Japan and borrows some characters from there, although their behaviour is purely my conjuring upon a footnote in history.

SHADOW PACK

*A tale from the today of 'These Pagan Isles' - a Britain
not quite as mundane as some would have us believe.*

The wolves of my youth are stalking me again. I used to see them, slinking from shadow to shadow, eyes like pale smoke, never quite there enough to make anyone believe me, but they were real enough. There wasn't a cat within three streets of my parent's house. On nights with no moon, small dogs 'wandered off' and pigeons apparently spontaneously exploded. Something to do with the electricity pylons, they said. So why did I always find feathers at my bedroom door each morning for three days, thirteen times a year?

I never feared the dark; I never feared strangers. There were always eyes in the shadows, there was always something about me that prevented anything interfering. Or should that be something near me?

One summer just after my fourteenth birthday, I met Chrissie. She was lovely and had those distractions that really matter to a growing lad. She was also the reason I started going to Sunday club and then to church. Always ready for a bit of fun but she hated staying out. Got really excited about it. Said something about 'the forces of darkness' and right then I decided that my furry visitors were not going to be a topic of conversation.

I would still see movements in the shadows but the presence had faded. I took to slipping out on moonless nights, just to feel them nearer to me. I never realised how much they had become a part of me. I would wait by the lamp-post at the edge of the waste ground, waiting for that moment when the silence became real and the sounds faded away. Then I would feel them. How I knew there were more than one I will never know, but they were many although I only ever saw one. I'm sure it was the same one: it would step delicately forward from the shadows, body silver and grey and I could see sharp contrasts through it when it stood still. It never came really close, but I got the feeling of - being questioned? Of being expected to know something? I never got it. Not then.

Things progressed and after three years Chrissie and I got engaged and she consented to letting things go further than kissing. It was after that first experience I got the pleasure of walking home in the rain, not caring about getting wet. Until I reached the lamp-post nearest my house. The wolf stepped out into the road opposite me, shining as the rain poured through it. It looked at me again, then turned and loped down the road a little way, toward the waste ground, then stopped and looked back, as if waiting for something. I smiled and then said the stupidest thing I have ever said to anyone: "Not tonight, boy. Gotta see Chrissie before work tomorrow."

It just stood, and I felt something slide down me, like a sheet sliding onto the floor. I looked down and there was nothing but wet pavement. I looked up and there was nothing but empty road. I ran the rest of the way home, the rain suddenly very cold and the night unfriendly.

That was it. No more night critters. Chrissie and I spent many happy years together, getting married on her twenty-first birthday. Our daughter Marianne was born exactly nine months later. Our son Luke was born a year after her.

On Luke's first birthday Marianne's kitten got into a fight with a fox and ended up as a gruesome patio decoration. She cried for days and no matter how many kittens or rescue cats we got after that, none stayed or survived more than a week. Chrissie was talking about exorcism but I stepped on that silliness hard.

On Luke's second birthday the neighbour's aviary was decimated by a rabid fox. We put up with weeks of roving pest control officers, animal rescue luminaries and reporters short on stock for the weekend edition.

On his third birthday I was woken very early in the morning by Chrissie screaming. Marianne had woken her. She had been bitten by something as she lay in her bed. At first I joked about hungry fleas until I saw the bruise on my daughter's arm. That was it. I went along with the whole series of events: doctors, police, social services, vicars, relatives. That was until I overheard one of Chrissie's grandparents muttering about some strange events in my youth to the deacon. At that point all my frustration at the well-intentioned but utterly futile attentions of all and sundry burst forth in a short tirade that cleared the house in minutes.

By the time I had calmed down, Chrissie had made various telephone apologies and the kids were asleep. With crumpled newspapers strewn around their doors. But nothing further happened.

From just before Luke's fourth birthday I took to getting up early and removing the feathers from outside his door. That was until I had to spend a couple of weeks in Italy on business. I was rousted from a sound four star hotel bed sleep by Chrissie on the phone, screaming about huge black dogs being after our son and bloody feathers left outside Luke's door. My business trip ended in a whirlwind of emergency travel arrangements and a police escort from the airport.

Chrissie had been sedated by the time I got there. Her parents were discussing things with the police in hushed tones, while my parents sat on opposite sides of our dining room table, staring at anything except each other. The evening was strained and when everyone took their leave it turned strange as my dad grabbed my arm as he stood on the doorstep. With a look of pasty-faced fear, he whispered: "Never have pets. Never hurt him. Never let his sister pick on him. I'm sorry."

With that he fled down the path to my mum, who looked at me with eyes full of apology for a secret kept past its time as she hugged him so tight I could see the whites of her knuckles as she gripped his jacket.

So I started a disjointed half-life; maintaining a happy family and good job whilst simultaneously watching for any event that could trigger a wolf episode. How could I explain to Chrissie that they were only protecting him? She started to go to church on the way home from work. She insisted that Luke and Marianne went to Sunday Pre-school.

One night it was my turn to attend to the kids, and as I looked in on Luke I saw he was awake, his eyes liquid dark in the shadowed room. I slipped in quietly and gently chided him about being awake. He rolled over and I felt his full attention on me.

"They see what you're doing, you know."

I stopped breathing. Luke was six.

"They remember you. They were sad to see you go."

He rolled over and as far as I could tell, fell instantly asleep. I didn't sleep at all that night.

Two nights later: another midnight monologue.

"I made them promise to be secret, dad. They said only because it was you." And another sleepless night afterwards.

Things fell into a delicate balance: me watchful and Chrissie religious to the point that 'marital relations' only meant that the family was coming round.

My dad died on Luke's tenth birthday. I had trouble with that. I also had trouble with my mum going completely off the deep end. Raving about pacts with the devil and dad going out running on nights with no moon, coming back scratched and dirty with his clothes torn to pieces. Unfortunately, she arrived at the house when I was away for a couple of days. It was three hours before a neighbour heard the screeching and called the police. By which time Chrissie was curled in a ball with the kids clinging to her, having retreated to, and then locked themselves in, Marianne's bedroom.

I cleared up the mess again, and tried to restore the previous semblance of normalcy. But I caught Chrissie staring at Luke oddly on several occasions, and the content of her stare made me decide that home-working for a while was a very good idea.

By Luke's eleventh birthday, I had returned to working away from home, happy that my presence around the house for a few months had done wonders for family harmony.

At this point, you may have noticed that Marianne doesn't get mentioned very often. This is true and unfortunately was true in life as well. My quiet monitoring of Luke meant that she frequently got told off for just behaving like a big sister, while his picking on her went unseen. Remember that Luke, despite moments of startling maturity and having supernatural guardians, was just a boy. But a boy who could keep a completely straight face about what exactly happened to Billy the Bully when they went trick or treating: Billy ran away that night. All because Luke got a black eye. I must believe that. I must.

Marianne was a lovely girl, grown pretty like her mum but with my mum's rounder figure. She bloomed early and needed her parent's calm advice. That would be advice from "Mummy the Bible-basher" and "Daddy who only wanted a son". So she turned to school friends. First it was Jessica, queen of the cheerleaders and her mum Clarissa. After an incident involving Jessica's boyfriend that went all round the school but never reached adult attention, Marianne took the rebellion path and linked up with Carpathia the Goth and her mum Serena. They got on really well and I liked them. Chrissie hissed and spat about devil worship, but for the first time ever I raised my voice to her and told her that her beliefs were fine, but they did not mean that everyone else's beliefs were evil.

I really think that it would all have worked out. Marianne would have grown well under Serena's day to day advice and our occasional parental guidance attempts. Luke would have become a studious but outdoors type of lad; his mum's pride and joy. As for me: if I could just have had six months between having to perform actions more suited to some weird secret service, I would have been happy.

On her fifteenth birthday Marianne had an abortion while on a school trip in Prague and nearly died. We never did get the name of the father from her. Chrissie blamed Serena and forbade Marianne to see her. Then she banned Carpathia from the house. We had a month of screaming arguments about that. Marianne came into my room one night toward the end of that month. For once she looked like she hadn't been crying. She was pale and smiled weakly before giving me the first unsolicited hug in about three years. She pulled back and looked me straight in the eye.

"My evil brother explained some things to me. You are possibly the greatest and stupidest dad a girl could ever have."

I took a deep breath and then went for it: "So you believe him?"

She smiled: "Believe him? He took me down to the park and introduced me."

She looked down, embarrassed: "I wet myself, dad."

Chrissie gave us both a look as we wandered downstairs, still chuckling. On his fifteenth birthday, Luke very quietly told me that he was reluctantly convinced that he was gay. For some reason I had a moment of dread. But that passed as we planned on how to tell Chrissie. Finally we consulted Marianne, and then took a unanimous decision that cowardice was the best policy.

Meanwhile, Chrissie tried to get me to come to church more. I agreed we needed help, but suggested counselling. She finally went with me and in a two hour session of complete honesty, I finally realised that without noticing, we had drifted apart. So very, very far apart.

Who fell first I will never know. Suffice to say that after a barbeque at Serena's house, I ended up putting more than the chairs away in Serena's garage. A couple of weeks before that event, a fine upstanding church-goer called Michael had offered to help Chrissie with her 'crisis of faith'. So on the barbeque weekend, Chrissie was at a religious retreat in France.

Things were strained after that, especially when Chrissie informed me that Michael reckoned that a weekend away at a teenage sanctuary would do our children a world of good. I agreed, feeling guilty about Serena while simultaneously planning a weekend of bacchanalian debauchery with her. It was two fifteen on the Sunday morning when Marianne called me. She had taken two mobile phones with her, so when her mother confiscated the one she knew about, she had a back up. Michael and Chrissie were leaving with the children for France. Apparently paperwork would be delivered to me on Monday stating my various marital and religious shortfalls as the reason for the marriage failing. Marianne was cut off just after I heard Chrissie enter her room.

Her last words were: "Dad, come and get us! Please!"

I nearly pulled Serena out of her own bed in my haste to get moving. Carpathia nearly passed out as I hurtled down the stairs and out of the front door. I was on my doorstep when I realised that I was naked except for my keys and a T-shirt that suggested that I 'bring my daughter to the slaughter'.

Several frantic phone calls later and I managed to successfully achieve nothing. As the sun set on Sunday I sat in an empty house watching the phone, willing it to ring.

Michael and Chrissie disappeared into Europe and no amount of money could find them. The legal niceties of our bitter divorce were handled by a solicitor in London, acting on behalf of a colleague in Paris. The private detective I hired saw Michael in Reims but was prevented from following by some people with Michael.

I will admit to losing it completely for a couple of months. Finally Serena took the simple solution and moved in along with Carpathia. My strident and self-pitying objections ended when I got the last of my wine poured over me as I lay on the floor clutching my testes.

Marianne phoned on her seventeenth birthday and I got a picture of them living in a rural religious commune somewhere in southern France. She was unhappy and said Luke was even more miserable as his guardians were causing havoc amongst the local farms. Serena had hidden all the alcoholic drinks before I finished the call. Then she and Carpathia sat and refused to move until I explained the cryptic references I had been using during the call.

Five months later I was interrupted in the middle of a meeting by a man from the government, informing me that my son had been injured in a shooting incident at a farm outside Toulouse. Despite Chrissie having achieved custody of the kids, he was refusing medical assistance until I was allowed to see him.

Four hours later I was in an unbelievably clean hospital, holding my son's hand while my daughter maintained a choke hold around my neck and cried continuously. Chrissie was standing in the doorway, Michael behind her and the French police behind him. Luke smiled at me, and whispered something. Moving Marianne around, I leant forward.

"I couldn't keep them bound, dad. They hated the place and the people. It was let them run or have a slaughter."

He looked me straight in the face and said: "Worse than Billy."

He coughed and blood hit my face. The nurse wiped us off and returned to her seat.

"They wanted to exorcise them. They knew I had something to do with them, so they took me out to a field and told me to call them. I wouldn't so Michael hit me. That brought them. The two priests held them at bay, but one of the farmers who'd lost a lot of his sheep got scared and shot me. It was a big gun, dad. After that, I really don't know what happened."

I did. Police had been called to the farm of a Monsieur Rapastian when a passing doctor saw a pack of dogs attacking people in a field. Although the police brought sharpshooters, no trace of the dogs were found. What they did find were seven dead members of a local commune and Michael cradling Luke against him, a knife held to my son's throat. He was screaming: "Keep back or I'll kill him!"

He kept on screaming that until one of the officers knocked him unconscious. But that delay was fatal. Luke had lost too much blood and internal injuries had leaked all manner of nastiness into places that it shouldn't be. The fact that he was still alive was only attributable to a miracle, according to the doctors.

As I sat there, crying quietly onto Marianne's head, Luke prodded his sister.

"Pay attention, twit. This is the good bit."

She looked up. They exchanged a smile.

"Dad, you can have them back. Just go outside, afterwards. But first, tell mum and the chickenshit homophobe that they will go with Marianne now. I think that they'll let sis go with you then."

He smiled and in it I saw many things that I just wouldn't have time to discover. With that, my boy just closed his eyes and left.

It took a while for me to stop crying, but I had a daughter to save. I laid
Marianne on the bed next door and dragged Michael over to where Chrissie
had collapsed in tears on the other side of Luke's bed. I gently but firmly
explained the problem about the pack and Marianne. As a beautiful
counterpoint, a mournful howl echoed outside the window. Chrissie and
Michael talked in hushed tones while police and marksmen ran around
outside looking for the rabid dog.

Eventually the furore died down and Chrissie finally agreed, aided, I think,
by Marianne's stream of awful threats in the background. I made a mental
note to have a word with that young lady about her language.

We left them there. Outside Marianne walked quickly across the car park,
nearly dragging me, saying that she had seen a playground down the road.
Sure enough it was there and so were they.

I had never seen the pack like this. There were at least two dozen. They lay
across the swings and lolled on the slides. As we approached they all came
to their feet, and three separated and came towards us. One I knew. The one
from my youth. It was bigger than I remembered. The other two came
nearer, the smaller stopping in front of Marianne, the other in front of me.
They both scratched the ground, but when Marianne reached down to stroke
it, her hand passed straight through. Then she stopped dead and in a really
quiet, shaky voice called: "Dad. Here."

I stepped over to her. She was slightly stooped, the three dimensional wolf
shadow by her still outstretched hand. With her other she pointed shakily at
the ground between them. In the packed earth was scratched four letters:

TWIT

I dropped to my knees. Looking at the insubstantial fur shining in a moon I
couldn't see, I took Marianne's hand.

"Luke?"

The wolf rolled over and then ran through the two of us. It was warm. And cold. And familiar. I had a sudden thought. I sprang over to the other wolf. In front of it was only three letters:

SON

We sat on the swings as the pack circled round. We sat there until the pack departed as the sun rose. They ran single file into the shadow of a rubbish bin and did not emerge from the other side. I took Marianne's hand.

"We will have a lot of explaining to do. And I think we need a house with a bigger garden."

I took my daughter home.

*

Epilogue

Marianne found this story in Eddie's (her dad's) things while she was helping me clear up after the funeral. I can't write as well as him, but this needs finishing properly.

When Eddie returned home with Marianne I was over the moon. I had been working with the coven to help him for months. Then the news of Luke's loss was delivered in entirely the wrong way. So Carpathia and I waited.

The following night I had a garden full of wolves. So I did what any of my kind would do. That weekend we had a barbeque, with a lot of extra meat and no bones left over.

Over the following ten years, Eddie and I researched his unusual family history. The tale is well lost, but here is what we feel is right, and what the pack disagrees with the least.

A long time ago, the goddess watched her consort lead the hunt for the worthy and the weak. For some time she had been aware that some crafters were focussing on only one aspect of the wheel, and most of them on the spiral ever down.

With the thought and the seeing came the actuality and the wolves rose to be. In balance their leader had to come from the middle land, a man from the apparent world.

The pack winnowed the craft, taking those too bound to one course. In the main, those were dark hearth and other dedicated shadow workers. But occasionally a light worker was taken, if they would have enforced pure light. For an entirety of anything will result in stagnation.

Sometime after the pack established itself, but in times still long ago, a group of shadow workers schemed to defend themselves from their bane. Unable to affect the pack, they went for the weakest link, the bloodline of the leader. A simple working or just the removal of a father before knowledge could be passed, and the pack were leaderless and could not hunt. But they knew their own, and over the centuries followed the strongest of the bloodlines, waiting, watching.

That is why Eddie has gone. The pack's leader has to willingly step from the middle land to lead them. Going in death is too late. Two moons ago Marianne, Carpathia and I buried a cardboard coffin filled with an Eddie-weight of fine compost that had an acorn in the middle.

In a room down the hall, Carpathia and Marianne are laughing with Conrad and Donald, their little brothers. There's a wolf shadow in their room already.

Eddie came to the circle on the first night of the full moon after he went. Nearly scared our waylock to death. He gave me this message to pass on:

Always it has been that to make a light is to cast a shadow.

Know that from the light you can make dark, but from the dark you cannot work light.

Beware your petty desires and dreams, for the spiral ever down is too easy to follow.

But should you fall, we will catch you.

If you have fallen, we will find you.

Should you have hidden, we will uncover you.

We are the shadowpack, and we will return you to the wheel.

My man stands outside the window as I write this, his grey cloak moving in a breeze from Niflheim as his wolves rise from the grey to fill our garden. His horns curve back over his head and his hair shines in the moonlight. His eyes blaze as he lifts his hand in greeting and farewell, again. Then they are gone.

***

UNDYING

A little while ago I got tangled in the first year of an online strategy war game. Whilst idly contemplating what sort of back story could possibly explain away the mechanics of the game, this tale emerged.

Kitty and Odelette were fighting again. Even looking out over a city filled with warbands all determined to out-party each other, he could hear them. The midsummer night simmered, only a few degrees cooler than the day. From the tower keep he could see the lights of Tareksburg to the south and knew that tonight it celebrated having a night without warbands carousing through its streets. A soprano scream of indignation cut his musings. Damn, he had better intervene soon. Spinning on the ball of his foot, Reon leapt to the stairway and took the stairs three at a time. Mareksburg was awash with warriors, all partying like tomorrow was the end of the world. Which it could be, for them. The townsfolk joined in or hid as their natures decreed.

Moving swiftly across the square Reon quickly acquired an escort of swordsmen and companions. Ogden, the massive hillman, and Merlin, the monk turned marauder, broke off their game of dara to accompany him. To one side he saw another group making for the ruckus.

A cheerful cry of: "A hundred gold on the brunette!" identified their leader as Sephnix Honourbound, visiting Lord and ally. As they entered the tavern quarter, the swordsmen cleared a path to the edge of the 'Headhunter' inn's grounds where the smiling, youthful countenance of Lord Kelvan Numerator greeted them.

"I make it three falls and one halter top to two falls and one loincloth."

Reon sighed as he put his hand over his eyes. Bracing himself, he stepped into the impromptu arena.

"Ladies, please! The men need to sleep tonight!"

Kitty straightened from a crouch and extended her arm toward a grinning trooper who dangled her halter from the hand that wasn't holding a beer. Pointing the other hand at Odelette, she spat: "That's no lady!"

Reon stepped back as Odelette lunged for her sister, to be brought up short by the heavily armoured form of Broderick, her second.

"Let me at her, the scheming cow!"

Broderick tilted his helmed head slightly and stood like a leaden statue until Odelette's shoulders dropped and she laid her off-hand on Broderick's chestplate. The move was strangely tender and once again Reon moved his opinion of the rumours regarding Odelette and Broderick from false to true. Odelette sighed: "Okay." She smiled as she turned to Reon: "Show's over, boss. Shame you missed it."

Kitty peered round Broderick: "If you tell the tin man to move, I can say hello to our beloved leader too."

Reon looked about. The troops were wandering off, the show being over and the impromptu gathering of a trio of Undying Lords and their companions discomfiting them. Sephnix watched appreciatively as Kitty and Odelette helped to straighten each other's gear, which they accomplished by the simple expedient of stripping naked and starting from scratch.

"Always like this?"

He enquired without shifting his gaze. Reon smiled. The sisters did make a lovely sight. But the day he had met them, they had been in a similar state of undress and covered in the blood of the men who had tried to violate them. Nine men killed bare-handed and the majority with their throats torn out by the same teeth that were now seen white and even when the sisters laughed as they dressed. Since that day, his thoughts never strayed toward desire with those two.

"Yup. Every time they spend more than a day in the same city and weekly thereafter. Which is why they're rostered in separate cities."

Kelvan wandered over, passing a hefty bag of coins to one of his escort.

"Many bet that the sisters would be naked before you stopped them. They lost."

Reon looked up at the sky, its deep shade of blue giving way to black. Far to the west, he could see a huge mass of dark clouds moving in.

"Let's adjourn to the keep before we get doused."

He crossed the threshold of the keep and turned to watch the Lords and companions gather. He could not help a grin as the sisters wandered by and in perfect synchrony blew him a kiss. He closed the oaken door and turned to the gathering, his smile vanishing.

"Right. You all know how this goes. Chard is Lord Kaisur's last city. This means he will be at his strongest and relying on the Pax to prevent us doing what needs to be done."

He watched as his people nodded. Now for the tricky bit.

"What I am about to say is fact. But you will never speak of it outside this room, ever. Am I understood?"

Their looks of curiosity were followed by nods. Reon smiled. His warlords. His companions.

"Lord Kaisur killed his Patron five months ago."

The looks of horror were unanimous.

"We are not sure how he achieved it. My Patron believes it was actually more opportunistic than planned, after that earthquake we had brought down part of the sanctum under Chard on its Patron. But whatever the reason, such blasphemy is intolerable and it also means one very important thing has changed."

Penny, the swordsmistress from lands far to the east, looked up from where she sharpened her scimitar.

"Lord Kaisur can be killed."

The others present looked back and forth as this revelation sank in. It was true. Without his Patron, Undying Lord Kaisur of Chard was actually nothing but a very dangerous mortal. Reon rapped the outer door to get their attention.

"Now you have the full picture, revise the battle plan. If Kaisur is slain, his troops will instantly sue for terms and enter our service. We will have to slaughter his companions as they are all as brutal as he is, but I see no reason to waste men and materiel when a surgical strike will save the day."

Kitty raised a mail-gloved hand. Reon nodded to her.

"Surgical strike is fine, but doing it through Chard's defences and two hundred thousand committed defenders is going to be a bit tricky."

Reon had been waiting for this. The next piece of news was even more shocking than the death of a Patron.

"My venerated Patron, Ashengyre, will be accompanying us. I do believe that may relieve the trickiness somewhat."

The looks were marvellous. Reon's eyes twinkled with glee as he managed to stun his folk again. His legend may have been orchestrated by his Patron, but it was now assured. He laughed out loud as he saw Penny mouth the word 'bastard' from the back of the group who were now chatting animatedly and beginning to pull charts from the shelves under the table. He moved to the stairs.

"I'll be in my rooms. Call when you have a revised plan."

Merlin called as he turned away.

"Forgive me, Undying Lord Reon Totemless."

Reon sighed. Old kingdom manners. He turned back and gestured for Merlin to speak.

"How big is your venerated Patron? It would be embarrassing for it to tread in our forces."

Reon pursed his lips, whistled and raised a hand to his head. A very good point. He thought about the sizes involved.

"Ashengyre would fit in Mareksburg from corner tower to corner tower only. You would need to demolish the wall from gateway to mid-tower to let her girth pass. That is from the gate tower on the opposite side to the mid-tower. If she needs to spread her wings, we will have to accept the casualties. Enough?"

Merlin bowed.

"Your venerated Patron is indeed the paragon of élan that drew us to serve you. The fact that she will sally with us on the morrow is proof of her pre-eminence."

Reon smiled. Merlin did courtly words with a natural delivery that defied him. The time for the main event had come quicker than she had predicted.

"Ashengyre will not be returning to her sanctum. She has decided that Chard will become her overlair. Plus she wishes to meet you all. We are to have the first risen Patron. Sephnix and Kelvan; please inform your Patrons that Ashengyre would convene all Patrons falling under our alliance as soon as Chard is taken. If the banner of Pyrefall is to spread across this land, then she expects every allied Patron to be overlaired. Indeed, it is to become a requirement of acceptance into Pyrefall. In her own words…"

His voice trailed off. She had her cue.

There shall be no more hiding behind our thralls.

Her words echoed through the minds of all present. With the exception of Reon, Sephnix and Kelvan, everyone either knelt or collapsed as their fortitude to mindspeech and being in the presence of legends in the making dictated. Reon grinned. Sephnix and Kelvan looked suitably impressed. The fact she had spoken to all present should give them the necessary authenticity when communicating with their Patrons. Reon beat a hasty retreat as he noted Sephnix and Kelvan take their leave. It would be better to let them plan and talk about such momentous events without Undying Lords being present.

The rainstorm had passed over by the time that he was disturbed from his readings by a knock at the door. At his call, Penny entered quickly then closed and secured the door before rapidly shedding her weapons, harness, armour and clothing. She leapt onto the bed where he lay with a whoop of joy.

"You did it! They are absolutely taken with the idea of dragons being up in the light."

Reon smiled and pulled her to him. She placed a restraining hand on his chest and poked him in the ribs. Reon grunted.

"Exactly where am I going to find a quiet place to shift into the immense form you described to Merlin? The poor companion's beside himself with eagerness and terror."

"The lake five miles due east is big enough. Change on the near shore."

"And why so big? I'm going to be positively cumbersome."

Reon chuckled before regarding her with a calm gaze.

"This is an event. This will spawn legends and tales for folk to pass down to their children. Plus I figured that if you're that damn big, no matter how many dragons the people see afterwards, the first thought and number one reply will be that they are nowhere near as big as Ashengyre."

She smiled and his heart thudded.

"You are a man occasionally blessed with moments of prescience that cut to the heart of things."

Reon raised a hand like a child before his tutor: "Dare I ask what I am for the rest of the time?"

She knelt and raised her hand, counting off items on her fingers as she spoke: "Always good for a free meal. Competent in bed. Making me see the humour and beauty around me. Being the one thing I would burn this planet to ashes for."

Reon took a sharp breath. That last one had been said with an intensity that almost scalded him as her eyes had blazed. He caressed her shoulders until she relaxed.

"You've all spent too long hiding in the dark. Well, not you. But your kindred have. It is time for them to join you in the joys of the land under the sun."

Pennishengyre, known to everyone else as either Ashengyre of Mareksburg, Matriarch of the Pyrefall Alliance or Penny the swordsmistress, smiled a huge smile as she grew a prehensile tail and gossamer wings.

"Indeed they have. Although I do suspect that Broderick is far more than the unstoppable hero and devoted companion of Odelette that rumours paint him to be."

Reon held her at arms length, raising his eyebrows.

"Broderick? Really?"

Pennishengyre furled her wings and settled in Reon's arms. She looked up and back with a mischievous smile.

"Odelette and Kitty have knifed him at least six times after consummating their quirky little relationship to my knowledge. He's a remarkably dangerous and healthy warrior for a dead man. My bet is that he's actually Theridion of Shipra, Sephnix's venerated Patron."

Reon whistled.

"Damn. How many more of your kin have been quietly shape-changing in violation of the Pax to get away from this tiresome, neverending war game, I wonder?"

Pennishengyre kissed his chest.

"Sadly very few. Taking Pyrefall overground should give them the impetus they need."

Reon stroked her hair as he looked out the window into the night.

"Do you think we'll be able to stop this insanity soon? So many deaths to alleviate the boredom of ageless children. It would be good to try for an actual civilisation."

She wrapped her tail around him intimately.

"Yes. They will swiftly lose their taste for second-hand bloodshed and intrigue when they discover the other… experiences that the overground offers."

Reon smiled as he felt himself respond to her voice dropping an octave.

"Damn. I never thought that the delights of drinking and farming would be so attractive to great drakes."

Pennishengyre slapped him hard as she laughed.

"Darling fool man. It is the loss of their loneliness that will change them."

She paused: "Although I do believe drinking will feature heavily at the start."

***

ANDEO

*A tale from the world of 'These Pagan Isles' - a place
not quite as mundane as some would have us believe.*

*As this tale contains a lot of acronyms, military slang
and foreign language, there is a glossary at the end.*

I never understood that grey was more than just a colour until I got there. Grey people fighting under a grey sky in the ruins of a grey city for assorted grey motives, while grey-skinned old boys sat with the grey-eyed shell-shocked around open fires that gave off wispy grey smoke. The mud was grey-brown and any liquid picked up the dust from the ruins to display grey swirls. Ubiquitous, Skinner called it. Good word: I'll be buggered if I can remember exactly what it means.

The niceties of the NATO intervention eluded most of the lads at the sharp end. We were too busy dealing with the day to day necessities of not getting frozen or dead or both in a war zone that seemed to suck the colour out of everything, including life if you weren't careful. The wet got you first, then the cold, and finally the grey arrived to do you in. That was when you needed your mates around, to remind you that over the artillery-infested hills was a colourful place of warmth and women and all you had to do was let the training hold it all off until the day you could make the transport out.

As 'agents of intervention' we were the spanners in everybody's machine; from the local grocer selling mouldy turnips around the remains of the truck that destroyed his shop front a few weeks back to the barely teenage soldiers who ran for the local gangs. The shopkeeper was alright; you could banter and barter with him. A thirteen year old with an AK-47 and no education was a different matter. Make him look small in his eyes by talking of anything he didn't understand or sympathise with, and he'd shoot you down as his first response.

The place had emptiness about it: a waiting for the next grim incident that really played you up on stag. Around the base quiet was the norm, apart from the inevitable ruckus of an active military base, but after a while you tuned it out to realise that apart from the noise your lot were making, there was nothing else. I grew up on a Norfolk farm, so I'm used to quiet. But that was something else. The only other thing that the two places have in common are the ravens. Although the ones there were bigger. Bloody great cheeky scavengers with sarcastic cawing and the ability to fly through anything to nab unguarded nibbles. The squad set up obstacle courses for them and we watched in astonishment as they flew, hopped, hovered and used bits of metal or twigs to lever their way to the reward. Amazing and slightly scary to realise that when one of those feathered lads looked at you, there was something smart behind that shiny stare. My mum always said that if I was 'deeply troubled' I should "Let the ravens take it". Which as far as I could work out at the time, meant tying your problems to a big black bird and letting the poor dumb bugger have 'em. Didn't seem fair then, and after I knew they weren't dumb at all it seemed like something plain wrong.

I held that opinion until I'd done a couple of clean-ups there. Bodies dismembered for their valuables left in blasted homes scavenged clean within minutes of the gunfire stopping. The sheer callous speed of it was breathtaking. Then one morning, as watery sunlight showed me too much detail again, I heard a movement.

The world went into slow motion as I stepped back and away while bringing my SA80 to bear. Time caught up again as the raven perched on top of the wall cocked its head at me, eyes giving back nothing but reflections.

My whispered "Bloody hell" sounded loud as I felt a smile spread across my face: wasting a beaky would get me hacked on for weeks. Then I felt strange, like the damn bird wanted something. Looking around the room at the mortal ruins, I felt my guts churn as a throbbing started behind my eyes. I looked up at that raven and whispered the words my mum had nagged into me: "It's yours. Take it and make something good."

With a low caw it hopped down onto the ruined dresser and started to look about like it was shopping. That did it. I shook myself out of the odd mood and booked back to the squad. From that day on I looked for the ravens, seeing them as some weird promise of better to come. Not that I told anyone, but the lads noticed. I put up with a couple of weeks of shit before coming clean: "I dunno, my mum always said them birds had something to see, like they was recce for something big to decide who gets it. So I figured that rather than feel like puking most of the time, I'd let the ravens have it to make sure some fucker gets his for turning this place into a shithole. Someone should answer for this mess."

Sergeant Andrews nodded his head, "Whatever gets you by, Jensen. Whatever gets you by."

But a couple of the other lads had a word later over a brew. They'd remarked on the number of the big dark birds just watching things. Kristof, the local liaison and bolt-on Bravo squad member, said that round here they were either good luck or bad, but never neutral. They also seemed to like the 28th. Wherever Bravo squad of the Royal Gloucestershire, Berkshire and Wiltshire Regiment went it was noted that ravens were always nearby and seemed to be accompanying the patrols.

Apart from that, the squad just got on with it. It cost me three months paper for decent kit, as the regular issue was anywhere between useless and a liability. The local Viper Tactical reps loved UK troops, but they loved the UK government more for putting us in at the proverbial deep end with only a rubber duck and a brick.

*

We'd been in Sarajevo for six months when the rumours that had been circulating made it into the intel feeds. Command wanted any and all information on a new gang, known as Andeli Upaklu - which translated as nonsense, although Kristof said it could be loosely interpreted as Hell's Angels. A name that made us glance at each other; images of fat bikers riding through this urban wasteland in a Mad Max rerun were enough for several hours of crap jokes.

It was three days after that I failed to absent himself quickly enough from Sarge's sight and got tagged for a news patrol. At best it was an afternoon of skulking about with your back itching from the shot that could come at any moment; all the while keeping the minty fresh reporter and his gung-ho cameraman from getting dead or causing an incident. At worst, it was an invite to be used as range practice by every variety of trigger-happy local.

We were two hours in and only lightly frazzled when all hell broke loose. As far as we could tell, we turned a corner and the two sides set up in a standoff each decided that we were reinforcements for the other team. End result: they all opened up on the PBI. It went pear-shaped fast: minty fresh reporter becoming good-looking corpse double quick, while gung-ho cameraman fell foul of the local ROE - if one of the opposition has a shoulder mounted anything, slot him first.

Suddenly we were seven lads, no civvies; huddled in ruins that amounted to about a quarter of a small house while Sarajevo howled and hammered at our disintegrating cover. An air strike was out of the question, backup had rolled out but was being held up by teenagers with RPGs and no concept of being outgunned.

Daffy, our Lance, had stopped something large calibre in the face as he went for a looksee; then Grim took two of the same: one in the throat and one through the comms pack as he spun out. Skinner had only taken a deep slice in the arm, thankfully his offside. He was binding it as best he could while quietly working his way through the sexual shortcomings of the ancestors of the knob that shot him when he suddenly bounced up onto his feet, SA80 aimed at the floor.

"There's some fucker under the boards!"

The last thing we needed was mates of the goons outside popping up in our very small hidey-hole. Skinner lumped the floor a few times, splintering wood, teeth bared. As he ripped out a charred board, a pair of small hands shot into view and a child's voice shouted something unintelligible in one of the local dialects. Skinner aimed his SA80 into the gap and flicked its spot on and off. Then he froze before looking up, an expression of horror on his face: "Oh Christ, there's a cellar stuffed with kids and teddy bears down here, Corp."

Corp looked like we all felt. Kids. In this? All of a sudden our survival chances dropped. But no way were this squad of Gloucesters booking without the little 'uns.

In amongst all this, a couple of the knobs from the side nearest to us got by Flinty, and suddenly we heard boots on the rubble on the other side of the wall. I hate flankers. If you're gonna go it shouldn't be to some sneaky knob without the decency to charge straight down the range at you.

We were just sorting ourselves to deal when all that came over the wall was a lot of someone else's blood. Arterial nothing, this was like the poor knob out there stepped on something primed in Czech and wrapped in ballbearings; Jesus, what a mess. We yelled, the kids screamed, Kristof ripped off a half mag over the front wall to keep the rest of the bleeders from getting any silly ideas; then this skinny bint in black and white fatigues hurtled over the wall, decked Skinner with an elbow, took Flinty in the balls with a sidekick; landed pretty as you please and suddenly I'm staring into the palest blue eyes down the length of what seemed to be a couple of yards of gore smeared sword. Corp was just levelling his

Browning when he took a half brick in the face from her offhand. Christ but she could move, her eyes never shifted from me as she threw it. She completed her arrival by rattling off a short phrase in half a dozen flavours of the local patois. I had no idea what she said but Kristof was suddenly babbling like he'd mainlined something pure. She blinked and her head swivelled inhumanly fast, seemingly checking our positions and ready states.

With a move that I was sure couldn't be done, at least not that smoothly and at that speed, her sword went from my very tender adam's apple into the sheath on her back. Then she shouted something over the wall. All the firing stopped. I caught the words "Andeli Upaklu" and decided that very still was a good thing to be. From the sudden silence, it seemed that everything within hearing range of her agreed.

She straightened up a bit and smiled. My life, but she went from mad sword-wielding bint to babe quickly.

"Am sorry. Thought you were locals. Some like children for easy money and worse."

Skinner rolled to his knees and smiled as he saw Flinty trying to put his balls back in the sack by the look of it; one hand shoved down the front of his pants, a look of pained concentration on his face. He shot a glance at her before turning to Corp.

"Bloody hell, love. Way to get our attention. You okay, Corp?"

The reply was a muffled grunt as Corp used a rag to sop his nose while rummaging for something to act as corks. Quik-clot is not for nosebleeds. Makes your eyes water a lot. Plus it hurts like a bastard snorting enough of it. Flinty looked up, his groin manipulation apparently complete.

"Good hit, darlin'. What happens now?"

"Take children. Leave."

Corp spat and wiped his cheeks and chin.

"I suppose that the trigger-happy dickheads are just going to let us go?"

She looked round at him and that smile seemed to get to Corp as well.

"They will if am with you. Very few will anger the people."

Something struck me as odd.

"Why? You work for some local warlord then?"

Her head snapped round to me, smile gone and eyes frosty again.

"And while I'm asking, where the fuck did you appear from and how did you know the kids were here?"

She smiled again. Damn. No fair and she knew it.

"Am working for me and mine. Have interests here. One is making sure few innocents get hurt. For that, people love us. Warlords and men find it difficult to live when the food vanishes, safe houses go and contacts are silent."

I looked across at Corp, raising my eyebrows in query. Corp shook his head resignedly.

"Bollocks to it. She says we walk with the kids, we walk with the kids. At least we can take Grim and Daffy with us. It's not like we were going anywhere but down here."

Corp smiled at her: "Just in case. I'm Corporal Teaks, mister balls-ache there is Flinty, bleeding arm is Skinner, looking confused while staring at your boobs is Jensen and our local fast talker is Kristof."

I went red as the smiles went round. She just stared pointedly at my crotch before looking at Corp and saying: "Call me Ruza."

She then offered to tidy Skinner's dressing as we had two bodies to lug for possibly a very long walk. When she finished Skinner actually looked impressed as he worked his arm.

"Bloody marvellous. Feels like I can juggle again."

She laughed quietly.

"Will hurt tonight, be fine in morning."

A few minutes later, we're part of a ragged column: fifteen kids, all under four foot tall, the bigger ones carrying the smaller, with at least two squads of grimy teddy bears clutched tight in every spare hand. Me and Skinner carrying Grim, Corp and Kristof lugging Daffy, leaving Flinty with the LSW for cover in case someone got hot and tried to start something. Ruza took point and Flinty was Tail-end charlie. I really thought we were actually going to make it out of Dodge when Ruza did a front somersault and went down like a sack of spuds as a muffled thud rang out behind us. Sniper! Flinty did what he did best, working out in moments approximately where the bugger was holed up and hosing the general area with dedication and venom. No-one could figure out how he did it, but it had saved a lot of people over the years, so we just let him get on with it. Cartridges spun and glinted in the late afternoon sun as I legged it forward to Ruza.

Hollywood just cannot bring itself to show sniper victims properly. They won't be lying there with a neat hole in them. If you're lucky there will be a big bit. If not, you'll need a shovel and a sack.

At least she was intact. I could see a big dark patch high on her back, but as I got nearer, she rolled over, cursing in a language I had never heard. Whatever armour she had on under those fatigues, I wanted some. She sat up and looked straight at me.

"Run. Get everyone out. The *bikkja* is mine."

With that, she took off like an Olympic sprinter toward the three storey that Flinty was just finishing emptying a second mag into. I looked at Corp.

"She says book with the kids, Corp."

"She'd be damn straight. Mount up! Flinty, point and watch our backs as we come up."

That was not a fun trip. Sniper knob had started something, and we spent a harrowing half hour dodging local colour until two Saxons rolled up with Charlie and Delta squads on board. After pasting the locals with some of our nastiest we all got the hell out of there.

*

It was next morning when Skinner woke me from a lovely coma with a brew: good lad. He had a smoke in his hand. I noticed because it was shaking. I shrugged my rigs and vest on before sinking half the cup. Then I looked at Skinner properly and saw he was pale.

"Arm giving you gyp, mate?"

Skinner lifted his arm and shook his head.

"No fear. The medic just threw me out coz my arm is fine. It's like I got a graze instead of the bleeder you saw yesterday. You did see it, didn't you?"

I'd seen it all right. Something about the calibre that took Grim and Daffy down had passed about a half-inch too close, and Skinner had a tear across his left bicep you could lay your finger in. The claret pissing out had been genuine too. It had soaked the arm of his jacket.

Skinner shucked his top. His arm had a little red mark where the wound had been. Like a four-inch paper cut a week after it happened.

"What the fuck happened, Jensen?"

I just stared at his arm. In my mind's eye I saw Ruza binding his arm after soaking the pad in something from a little bottle that had appeared from one of her pockets.

"We got had mate. She's a bird from some sort of special projects mob."

"I checked. No-one has a clue about her and nobody is owning up to any girlies with big swords and marching powder reaction times. Let alone anyone who could take a sniper hit square on and then sprint a quarter-mile to have a word with the bugger."

"If they were testing some weaponised PCP, they wouldn't admit it."

"True."

Skinner grinned. "Shame. She had a nice arse."

I grinned back and we loaded up for the day.

*

That's how it went. Days of boredom, days of near death. Always grey and always ravens nearby. So much so that Bravo squad got a new name: 'Twitchers'. Wherever we went the birds were there. Started to get even weirder when we noticed that a caw from nearby meant we were about to get something interesting incoming from that direction.

After a month or so of this I started to keep a notebook about the weird shit that was going down. Skinner suggested we start asking the lads we met about anything odd. Then he paused before reluctantly saying, "We should see if anyone else has seen this Ruza bint."

Command was getting quite loud about info on the Andeli Upaklu and, when me and Skinner started getting nosey, we found that Ruza was considered to be one of them, and a 'person of interest'. The report on our little excursion was classified double-quick and we were pointedly informed that discussing anything about her was bad form. So, naturally, we carried on doing our job and asking questions when time and mayhem allowed.

A couple of weeks later, we had a natter with some special ops boys who were decent enough to chat with us commoners. We found that Ruza was known to them by name. She had saved one of their team during a night op when the berk tripped a wire and got jumped on by something nasty. Now I know troops talk up incidents, especially situations where they only get out by applied fury. But these lads were insistent that whatever their boy had alerted threw him thirty feet, through a wall. He was well shagged over when out of nowhere, Ruza came through "like an HST" and planted both feet in the hostile's gut, punching him through a window and a lot further, if the sounds were anything to go by. Then she pulls their lad out of the rubble he created, checks him over, massages his neck and the lad is good to run. Nasty had done a runner as they couldn't find his body, and when they came back, she had exchanged some intel with their lead man and then buggered off into the night.

They also knew the name of another one of her mob: a similar spec bint calling herself Svila. She had popped up a couple of weeks after Ruza, when a team found a truckload of teenagers being driven out of town on one of the roads to the rebel strongholds. It all got a bit frantic when a rebel APC rolled into the mix and one of the teens, a girl, started screaming something into the night after her brother or boyfriend stopped a lot of bullets by throwing himself across her. Next thing, there's a bloody great flash and the APC is a rolling crematorium and in comes Svila, slicing up bad guys and generally screaming blue murder in some language nobody understood. After the dust settles, she stays long enough to turn a couple of stretcher cases into walking wounded and have a word with the kids - especially the girl who screamed; then she takes off into the undergrowth. Spooked the ops on the run because all the teenagers suddenly knelt down and started praying in the direction she went off in. Then they got up and things progressed a little more like how you'd expect a bunch of kidnapped teens saved by the good guys to progress.

Skinner and I were on to something, but one thing we realised pretty quick was that Command were not playing nicey-nicey over this. A nurse who occasionally humped Skinner told him that the girl who lost her brother went off with some very hard types, possibly 'private security' – a polite term for mercenaries who worked for whichever bleeder could stump up enough dosh to afford 'em. Which was not usually anyone completely above board.

So we kept quiet and soldiered on some more. By the start of the New Year we had a very odd picture to think over. Of course, we brought in all of Bravo over it, including our two new members: Rally and Swift. Skinner knew Rally from way back, so Corp had called in a couple of markers to get him, and Swift was fresh from something dark in Gorazde.

It seemed that 'our' Ruza was regarded as the leader of a small group of women who spent their time making sure the local civvies did not get savaged by the arseholes using their city as a war zone. They were pretty impartial, too. We had a couple of tales of her mob mixing it with our side as well; when a couple of the lads from the Fusiliers got a bit handy with some barkeep, and more interestingly when some of these 'private security' bods had tried to make off with an old boy from Drugi Dom, the only café that served the locals and our lot.

While I did the writing, Skinner did the math. He reckoned that Ruza's mob was squad sized at best: maybe a dozen tops. Hard as nails, faster than everyone else and damn near worshipped by the locals. Still only had one other name though: Svila. Nobody had any idea where they holed up either, but in the mess that Sarajevo had become that was no real surprise.

I had an idea and suggested we take a meet and greet down to the Dom and if we happened to meet the old boy, we could ask him why the goon squad had been after him. Kristof was up for it and only Corp had reservations, but a quick word with Sarge and we were good to go as he got points from on high for coming up with such a fine 'publicity and relations' opportunity. Two days later we got an evening pass to go meet the locals and be nice, Command were delighted at the possibility for good press, which meant we got a berk named Graffon to act as our liaison so the PBI didn't tell the truth and embarrass anyone. He and Kristof were spitting like tomcats within seconds of meeting each other.

We were having a decent outing, all the locals were on best behaviour as well, the newshounds were lapping it up, then some knob stuffed a RPG into one of our Landies parked across the road while his mates put a couple of rounds through the window of the café for good measure. Of course, that divided us. The locals were screaming and diving, all of Bravo squad scrambling to get their kit and get outside, the newshounds were drooling and having to be slapped down to let the boys with the guns out first, the usual chaos. I was a tardy Tail-end charlie as I'd been chatting up the owner's daughter, so I was just about to go out the door when I heard the locals take it up a notch. I spun round expecting a local gangbanger and instead I was looking down an H&K in the hands of one of the private security goons. I had dropped my SA80 back to port and was raising an arm to point him out the door toward the bad guys when the fucker shot me. "Short burst, low gut shot, lovely job," was my last thought as I felt a big invisible hammer punch my arse backwards and my head came down on the table so hard it folded around my ears. I was out for the count before I completed crashing to the floor.

*

I came back to the lovely sound of a full blown firefight. It was music, 'cause I'm pretty sure heaven doesn't issue AK-47s, which meant I hadn't had my card punched. I opened an eye to find a pert left buttock just within biting range, as Flinty would have said. Said butt was wrapped in black and white camo and the owner of it was doing something freaky with my guts. I was all warm and cold and tingly down where I'd taken the hit. As I thought it, my saviour sat up and looked back over her shoulder at me.

"*Kvedja*, Jensen."

Ruza smiled as she wiped her hands on my trews.

"You will hurt a lot tomorrow but will be good."

I found my voice after spitting something grim onto the floor.

"I thought I'd copped it. Ta."

As she started to stand up my hands were already reaching for my SA80. She put a hand on my head.

"Tonight you are *vardmadr*, Jensen *gildr*. You stay put, let others fight."

When I tried to sit up, I felt my lower guts move in a way they shouldn't, so lay back down sharpish.

"Okay. I'll be vardmadder, whatever that is."

Ruza grinned a berserker grin, a savage thing to see on a pretty face.

"Watcher, it means watcher. Now stay."

With that, she was out the back door.

So I lay there as Sarajevo yowled and threw things outside. After a while the firefight moved away a bit and I heard a scraping. When I looked down, there was an old boy crawling my way, sliding a tray with two steaming cups of something on it. Things were looking up. He smiled at me and muttered something in Serbian. I shook my head and to my surprise, he replied in Oxford English.

"Tea, dear boy?"

"Too bloody right, pops. Thanks."

"It seemed the least I could do as you stopped the *strazar* from getting me again."

"What?"

"Literally it means guardsman. We use it to refer to any who work for *tama vlasnik*."

"Who?"

"Shadow lord. It is what we call the one who walks between the warlords, the government and your top brass with impunity."

"You mean there's some bugger working all sides in this? He must be making a fortune."

"Indeed. But not like you and I think. Ruza knows but she refuses to tell, just does her best to make sure he doesn't get it, as far as I can understand."

The night had finally fallen quiet outside. I sipped tea and chatted idly with the white-haired old gent, my back against a dresser and my boots under a table. That's where Skinner found us when he returned, leading a medic at double time. Said medic was not impressed.

"You said he was leaking like a sieve from a hole in his gut, Skinner. I should do you after the other morning's bollocks over your arm."

"I swear he was pissing claret and oozing green shit all over the place."

The medic looked back and forth between us and was about to say something when the old boy raised his cup in salute. Medico stomped off. Probably best not to need attention for a week or so unless dying, I thought. Skinner propped himself on the window ledge and cadged half of my cuppa.

"So, you get some of Ruza's medicine?"

"Dunno, mate. I was a bit out of it."

"Yes, he did."

We both stared at the old boy. Who raised an imaginary topper to us.

"Etherington Bailey, at your service."

Skinner smiled.

"Bailey? As in 'Dreams of Gods and Men', E.D.F. Bailey?"

Always knew he read too much for a squaddie. Etherington looked startled and then smiled.

"Delighted to meet an erudite scholar of the divine, dear boy. Yes, that little opus was mine."

Skinner shook his head.

"Had to read the bloody thing in R.E. as my teacher was a huge fan: Mister Bisford."

Etherington laughed.

"Ah, the eager Bisford finally settled in religious studies, eh? Silly sod, he could have done better."

Right, enough of this bollocks, I thought.

"Can we do the trip down memory lane later, chaps? I'm gonna need a hand and I think Mister Bailey needs to find a new watering hole for a while."

They had the grace to look abashed as they helped me up, then me and Skinner made for the Saxon as Etherington lit a cigarillo and strolled off into the night, looking like he hadn't a care in the world even after we recommended he make himself scarce for a bit. On the way back, I got Skinner to give me an update.

"We baled out front to see half a dozen locals with AKs pegging it down the road, so we went after them cautious like and sure enough they wanted us to walk into a meat grinder."

"So we scragged the lot of 'em with help from some Fusiliers who were rolling nearby, then we get a local screaming about men in black and you being shot. So I leg it back and sure enough, you're down with soup leaking out and Ruza is giving some bloke in stealth gear a right seeing too."

"Five and a half, H&K, plates and jacket?"

"That would be the one."

"I hope she chopped him a new one from the neck down."

"Dunno, mate. I clocked that she didn't need help, then rabbited for Swift to call the medicos in. I get back and you're havin' tea with a philosophy professor and she's gone and stealth goon is missing too."

I got looked over when we got back: medico said I'd just had a slipped plate punched into my groin by the shots. Nothing there but black, blue and tender with a couple of long red lines. Christ but I shit a bloody brick the next day after an agonising night. Felt like my guts were trying to get out under their own power.

*

After that, Command got real eager to find out why Ruza was so keen on Bravo squad. I spent a delightful afternoon having my morals, balls and loyalty questioned by some blokes in civvies who moved like Special Forces. When they finally realised I actually knew fuck all they sent me back to the squad. By then, we were all pissed in new and interesting ways. Some private security knob puts a few rounds in me and the brass are questioning Bravo? Something was rotten at the top. I had an idea and a short while after I had a chat with Corp about *tama vlasnik* he agreed and Bravo got itself a personal op: we wanted to know what these mercenary goons were playing at and we were not taking 'classified' as an answer.

Over the next three weeks we did the day to day at gung-ho speed so we could snatch time to sniff about and query anyone we felt we could trust. Turned out that these private security muppets were into everything and had access everywhere. Then Swift came up trumps when one of his old unit from Gorazde dropped by for a beer and left us with a souvenir of a recent nasty episode down his way. It was a knackered, twisted chunk of a SA80, but the intel tags on it said it had been taken from the opposition. The win was the serial and MOD sequence numbers. The lads in Gorazde had been strafed by weapons from our regimental store!

We went with Swift to Corp, who after hearing us out led us to Sarge, who said some truly choice words before calling division. We hit the sack that night well pleased.

Next day, Sarge was on us as we woke. He looked like he'd been force-fed lemons and his manner matched. He also had a Captain Dell riding herd on him. He mustered Bravo squad with a bellow and then carefully putting his back to the Captain, he rolled his eyes a lot while he delivered a nice little speech:

"Command says nice job, lads. Unfortunately you got the wrong end of the stick as the weapon found was part of an ongoing operation to catch some gunrunners operating in Sarajevo and Gorazde theatres. So it's top marks for the squad and let's get back to making this town safe again."

We were gobsmacked as Captain Dell stood behind Sarge and actually nodded his head, smiling as we were fed hot bullshit for breakfast. With that, they both departed rapidly, Captain Dell chatting happily about 'good work' and 'fine team' as he faded from sight and hearing. Half an hour later Sarge was back.

"Right, in case any of you missed the version for the hard of hearing, what I said earlier was utter bollocks. We caught someone with their fist in the tart and they do not like it one bit. Command is having a shit fit over this and they are looking for someone or a mob of someones to hang it on. So Bravo squad are going to be good lads and do some by the book soldiering for a while."

So we did. By the numbers we yomped through a fortnight of patrols and the usual waffle without a hitch and with no further visits from knobs in suits. It looked like we had gotten away with it, then week three arrived along with Captain Dell and some very special orders.

Next thing we know, Bravo had been seconded to some hair-brained patchwork outfit who were going to "take the battle to the rebels" and "bring some peace and safety to Sarajevo" by tabbing up into the hills and persuading the rebels to stop raining shit on us. You'd think from the press release we were going to go up there and talk 'em out of hostilities with a few bottles of the local spirit, a couple of games of cards and some good old camaraderie.

Like hell we were. The cobbled together company spent two weeks walking up one bloody hill and down the next one and all we found was where the buggers had been before they saw us coming. Of course, by the time we were up the second hill, they were back on the first one and raining shit down on the city as usual. It was a great game for them, and we got to look like prize idiots. Of course, in the time honoured tradition, when the Colonel in charge got it in the neck from the brass, he had a go at his team, they had a go at their teams, who came back and had a go at their squad leaders, so two days later our new Sarge was having a shit fit all over us because we hadn't learned how to fly between frigging hilltops just yet.

Unlike our feathered mates who had been surfing the updrafts and generally revelling in it, cawing down over our heads as if taking the piss while we slogged up another goat trail to nowhere.

Then Skinner had another idea, Corp tells Sarge, Sarge trots off all happy and suddenly the Slasher's Bravo, Charlie and Delta squads had been volunteered to put Skinner's completely barmy idea into action. We all decided that next time Skinner had an idea, he was going swimming in the latrine until he got over it. Charlie and Delta squads were extra impressed, having been scrambled from duty in the town to come and join us in our hillside shenanigans.

Next evening just after nightfall, the rest of the company moved off as it usually did, but it left us behind well dug in and pretending to be rocks, bushes and goatshit. It was a simple idea: when the rebels came to re-establish their fire base, we'd be waiting to give them a pasting.

Well, night turned to bloody cold early morning with no sign of the locals. By then we were damn near frozen in place and soaked through. I was wondering when the Sarge was going to call it in when Tanner, Charlie squad's scout, legs it across the open ground screaming something about claws. He was halfway across when a muffled thud coincided with his head exploding. The sniper knob from the crossfire incident was here!

We'd been clocked by the locals and were fucked in new and interesting ways over the next hour. Shit and derision, they had us tucked up nicely. While the artillery kept the company from coming back, the bleeders who had circled the hill outside our circle proceeded to have a duck shoot. They knew the ground, we couldn't even stand up without being silhouetted against the night sky: God what a mess. In the end, we got told to bust out however we could and make for the main group. Charlie Squad had taken a pasting, so their last three lads hooked up with us. The expanded Bravo Squad got its game face on, amped up the fury and went apeshit all over the way down. Flinty laid fire with two LSWs, Rally picked off anything stupid enough to stick itself out of cover, me and Skinner did bad things with CQC using Solingen steel and Brownings, Corp and Lance rained grenades down either side of our chosen route, and Kristof held the rear with a belt fed shotgun, ably backed by the Charlie Squad fire team. The autoshotty broke the ROE and sounded like a hammer of the gods, but that combined with the Minimi meant no bugger wanted to come up on us from the rear quarter. Or so we thought.

We were through the circle of bad guys and making our way right and down when Mack, gunner of the Charlie Squad fire team, started cursing as he hosed the hill up to our left.

"Hold still, you slippery motherfucker!"

I was nearest at the time, so I holstered my CQC gear, brought the SA80 up and moved across to back up Slips and Windy, Mack's buddies.

"What 'ave we got, Mack?"

"Something coming in fast and bloody good at not letting me hit 'im."

At which point Mack's head left his neck and I got a face full of Mack-flavoured claret as I was knocked down by his falling body. Which I am bloody sure saved my arse because whatever did for Mack thought he'd got me as well. I lay winded as a right ruckus kicked off to my right. I pushed Mack's corpse off me and wiped my eyes, then looked over, but the night hid everything except muzzle flashes that added a mad strobe effect to fuck up any chance of me seeing what the bloody hell was happening. I guessed that we'd blundered downhill into a group of the locals who took exception to us living any longer. The night was suddenly full of bullets and swearing in at least three languages. Silhouettes rushed through the night and blades glinted in more muzzle flashes. Then I heard someone screaming random English abuse until it stopped suddenly and something body weight rolled off down the hill. Who were these nutters? Scoping about, I heard Skinner swearing in the monotone he used when he was well pissed, so I headed for him, switching SA80 for CQC gear again, because this was going to be up close and very personal.

Sure enough, Skinner's standing over one of ours whose face is glistening craggy ruins in the occasional light and that's all I ever want to remember. Facing Skinner was a chunky type in lightweights, who seemed to be waving a couple of bloody big knives about and must have been well hard, because Skinner was spitting mad but not getting stuck in. I moved right, skipped the introductions and stuffed my knife into the side of Chunky's neck, all the way to the hilt in one, while my other hand rammed the

Browning into his kidneys before letting off three rapid. I finished with a solid boot to the back of his right knee and Chunky went down fast.

Skinner just stood there shaking. I grabbed him and was about to drag him away when someone shoved a red-hot poker clean through my right thigh and into my nuts. I heard a noise like a soprano pig and realised it came from me as Chunky, on his knees, claret hosing from his neck, stuffed his other claw into my groin. Yes, I said claw. The middle fingers of each hand were over a foot long and bone white. Chunky smiled at me and I saw his teeth were filed to points. No, pointed. They were all pointed. Then Skinner shoved his Browning into that smile hard and pulled the trigger as fast as he could. Chunky flew backwards, natty dentistry ruined but unfortunately that move explosively removed his mutant digits from me. The pain was bright and hot and then oblivion jumped me.

*

Skinner got put up for a gong for getting me out of there. Twelve miles and seven days through hostile territory with me over his back or leaning on him. Truth is, he refused it because we didn't get out. We were rescued.

*

Skinner says he was shitting it when he saw what Chunky was using for blades. Then I waded in and he just went in to save his mate. He's trying to stop essential bits of me spurting out of the bloody great hole in my groin when Kristof arrived just in time to put Chunky down *again* with half a dozen rounds of 12 gauge solid. Within a few minutes, we had Bravo Squad, battered, bloody but still up for a scrap around us and the god-knows-whats were coming in to finish the job. It would have been a punch-up of epic proportions if one of their own artillery hadn't dropped one short.

In Skinner's own words: "We were fucked but bloody sure they were gonna bleed before they took us. They came in a rush; blades, teeth, claws and all the horror flick trimmings as I heard incoming. I shouted to the lads to drop and then it all went bang."

Thankfully the shell was only high explosive, but it was big. The rest of Bravo got chucked down the hill and managed to make it out with most of their limbs and some interesting stories that they'll never dare tell their grandchildren. Me and Skinner got blown clean off the side of the hill and down into a wooded defile that still has no name on any map I've seen. A hundred foot drop on to pointy trees and lumpy rocks. Skinner says his last thoughts were that they'd never find our bodies.

I came round in the evening to the caw of a raven. He was up in one of the ragged trees and looked so healthy I hated him. I felt like shit and death reheated. My first few words were directed at no one in particular but I meant them with every ounce of my busted, aching body.

"Easy, Jensen. We're good."

Bloody hell, Skinner's voice was the last thing I expected to hear. I sat up quick, saw him start toward me as a hand fell on my shoulder; too late. The pain inside tore my awake apart.

I came round for the second time and I was propped up against a rock. The little clearing was dimly seen through the purple haze of late evening. Skinner sat opposite me. He looked like shit. Which meant I looked worse. Then I saw what was sitting pretty on the rock outcrop next to him. She looked like Ruza, with paler hair and wings. Wings? Too much, too soon. I blacked out again.

Third time lucky, as they say. I was still against the rock and it was still evening. Skinner was still opposite me, but thankfully my hallucination had left. Skinner was grinning at me.

"Now, you going to stay with us?"

"Fuck off, Skinner. I thought I saw some battle angel on the rock next to you and it was a bit much."

Skinner glanced to my left, behind me. Oh, no. There was a metallic rustling and Ruza leaned into view from above. She smiled. Yup, that still worked.

"*Kvedja*, Jensen."

"Hi."

"Feel better? Need to talk, not easy if you faint again."

"I'm good."

Ruza disappeared from view and I heard her climb off the rock I was propped against. Then she stepped round from my right. Her wings were furled and glinted in the dim light. She smiled again as the vision I'd seen perched next to Skinner stepped into view from my left, pale hair drifting slowly in the faint breeze of her wings settling. I smiled, whispered "Sorry" and blacked out again.

The next time I came back, it was thankfully still evening and I could look at the two of them crouched and chatting idly with Skinner without throwing up or screaming myself unconscious. As none of 'em had noticed my eyes open, I just stared for a bit. Their wings weren't actually feathered, more like sheets of very fine metal that moved independently of each other, making soft metallic noises as they moved.

Both of them had short skirts of a dark material set with metal discs, with their legs clad in incredibly fine mesh leggings that disappeared into their dark knee high boots. Across their backs, between the wings, their swords were scabbarded. Their upper bodies were fronted with metallic bodyform armour, that left their backs bare except for a complex webbing of the dark material that left their wings free to move. They had steel shoulder pads that left their upper arms bare except for the double twist of cloth around each bicep. Their hands and forearms were enclosed in gloves of the same material as their leggings. Ruza's hair was near waist length and probably still auburn, while the other one's was very pale. I smiled. A platinum blonde battle angel. Skinner looked across at me and smiled.

"Hello, you lightweight. Anyone would think that seeing two babes with wings was unusual."

"Fuck off, you sarky git."

Skinner looked at Ruza.

"He's fine."

Ruza and her companion looked round at me. Ruza gestured to her pale haired companion.

"Svila."

"Pleased to meet you, 'scuse me if I don't get up."

Svila smiled. Oh God, she could do that too? Ruza said something low and Svila turned the wattage on her smile down a bit. I took a breath at last. Ruza came across to me and sat down, her legs crossed at the ankle, arms around knees as her wings spread a bit to keep her upright. Her pale blue eyes caught mine.

"Jensen. Sorry you got caught up in this, but you now have a decision to make."

I noticed her English was better all of a sudden. I stretched my legs carefully and looked back at her.

"Go on then."

"The *valravne* knows you work with me. He managed to get all of Svila's team, but up there he made a mistake. Too much trying and too many trying to help and prove their worth made a mess of his ambush."

"Val-ray-veen?"

"I will explain after I have explained your situation."

I nodded. It hurt.

"You are under my protection here, like Skinner is under Svila's. We can only extend this because you worked with the ravens and our lord likes that. So when I asked, he agreed. For a little while."

I must have looked as confused as I felt, because Skinner grinned like a lunatic.

"You're gonna love this, mate."

Ruza shot him a look as Svila tapped him sharply on the nose. His expression made me laugh. That hurt too. Ruza turned back to me.

"You died when the shell blew you over the edge and down here."

I looked at her. I must have misheard that.

"What?"

"You died. So did he."

She pointed at Skinner. I shook my head, slowly.

"So I'm dead and this is…"

I racked my memory.

"…Valhalla?"

Svila slapped her thigh with a shout of laughter. She then rattled off something to Ruza, who smiled as she replied with something short and I guess rude.

"No, this is not the Hall of Heroes. This is somewhere between, somewhere we can talk and you can decide and then it will be gone."

Must be something about being dead, but I was obviously missing something.

"Nope. I'm not getting this at all."

Skinner raised his hands in exasperation.

"Ruza, can I try in words small enough to get through?"

Ruza nodded her head as I called Skinner several names again. Then Skinner went all dead serious on me. He didn't do it often and I knew it meant no bullshit was coming.

"Jensen, mate. As far as I can grab from what these two have said, you're going to need to bear with me. Let me sketch it out and you can chuck questions after, alright?"

I nodded. Skinner shifted position and started in his finest lecturer's voice.

"Ruza and Svila are what used to be called Valkyries, the Choosers of the Slain. But as far as that goes, the entry requirements were a bit too lax after a while. Too many wars and too many atrocities commited by good men for what they perceived as good reasons. Some of the stupid buggers even turned on the Valkyries when they turned up to take them off to the Hall of Heroes. It seems the old gods don't actually distinguish between faiths. A brave, honest warrior is worthy regardless of which pantheon he or she follows. However, the converse is not true. Some of those good warriors become very unreasonable when devils, jinn, succubi or whatever their faith called them turned up to take them away from their just heavenly reward. Valkyries were *killed*, Jensen. Stupidity, blind faith and fear resulted in unholy tragedy."

Skinner paused and took a swig from a bottle.

"So, the top man upstairs decided that he needed to change with the times. The Hall of Heroes is still there for those who believe or can accept it. But for the rest, they go wherever the powers will. Let their gods reward them. His Valkyries have become 'choosers of the slain' more literally. In a world where heroes and good guys are fighting an uphill struggle, the Valkyries get to watch over the best and if they die in a shitty situation, they can revoke it. They choose who dies, not who's died. Apparently the bad guys have been getting the numbers for a very long time, so the good guys need quality. Oh, and the ability to ignore dying occasionally."

I looked at Skinner.

"So we're good guys? The best of the best? Bloody hell, mate. That's a stretch."

Ruza placed a finger on my forehead and a faint warmth radiated from her touch.

"You are good, Jensen. Deep down, regardless of what angers you, your soul stands watching a raven fly over autumn fields, just enjoying the sight of it."

I smiled. That memory was a favourite, true enough. Ruza took her finger away before speaking.

"The *valravne* knows you two. It knows your squad. It will try again. Next time it will kill you, or you must kill it. Which you cannot do without help."

"What the fuck is a val-ray-veen?"

"A raven that has eaten the heart of a slain king, back in the times when Valkyries would come for all royalty. It gained much; human knowledge, indefinite life if it fed on certain hearts, could assume human form if it consumed a child's heart, and has powers far beyond anything modern times can cope with. They are terrible animals and thankfully very rare."

"So chunky with the claw fingers was one?"

"No, he was just a favoured servant of it. You slew him three times, so he will not be back."

I put two and two together.

"This *valravne* thing is way worse, isn't it?"

Ruza looked at me and just nodded her head. Then she smiled.

"But with your squad and us, we can kill it."

"Hang on, you mean we get to do the resurrection shuffle? Full on Jesus thing?"

Ruza laughed.

"No, you are not yet dead. Your bodies lie in the ravine, not dead, not alive. Undecided. This is your decision. Will you return and fight a battle like no other to save so many who will never know and avenge so very many more? Or you can choose to go the Halls. You have earned the right."

I looked at Skinner. He smiled and I bloody knew he'd chosen already, and I knew what he'd chosen. We'd talked about getting the second chance many times. I looked up at Ruza and smiled.

"Spend forever in the original squaddie's club listening to drunken blokes boast about what they did? Not a chance. Send me back. This Bad Raven bloke needs plucking."

Ruza shouted something to the skies and Svila joined in. Then she knelt across my legs, grabbed me by the scalp and neck and kissed me, hard. It was...

Was...

Beyond description. Beyond anything. I blacked out again.

*

I came to slung over Skinner's shoulder with a lovely view of his right buttock through the monster rip in his pants.

"Fuck me Skinner, you going nudist on me?"

He crouched and let me stand before giving me the finger.

"I've just carried you two miles, you fat git. I'll undress how I like. Plus I got hung up on a savage thorn bush about a mile back."

Actually, we both felt pretty good considering what we'd been through. Guess joining the angels had other advantages as well as high voltage kissing. After a few minutes to redistribute our kit, we put ourselves in gear and tabbed off home. Took a while and I got shot again, but the knob was aiming for Skinner so it made us evens for the carry down the mountain. The worst moment was nearly getting slotted by a bunch of gung-ho Fusiliers before they realised we were the real deal. We both spent a week in hospital while a tedious number of people either pumped us full of drugs or pumped us for information. I don't think any of them did both. Either way, day eight and we were sent packing to make room for the poor buggers who really needed the beds.

Bravo squad were so pleased to see us they actually made us a cuppa after the Sarge had buggered off. When Flinty offered Skinner a smoke as well, we knew we were for it. Bravo had survived some strange shit and the two of us obviously knew what the fuck was going on. They wanted the lowdown and they wanted it now. I looked at Skinner. He looked at me and shrugged. So we told them the fucking lot. It took a while, but they said nothing until we were finished. Then Swift turned to Rally and asked:

"Does your mate always get the only good looking birds in the shitstorm?"

Rally shook his head, a grin forming.

"Nope. Skinner always bitches about Jensen getting the redheads."

That was the only comment. I turned to Skinner.

"Game on. How do we get Bad Raven to come out to play, smart lad?"

Kristof chimed in: "We take something he wants a lot. Or stop him getting it. Plus we make mess of anything of his we can find at same time. Make him angry. Make him want to come and tear our balls off. Make him so mad he don't think about plan."

Corporal Teaks slapped Kristof on the shoulder.

"For a local lad, you do East End ruck real well."

With that as a starter, we got stuck in. It wasn't easy, knowing that somewhere in Sarajevo a damn near immortal nasty was keen to have us dead and we had to move through its back yard every day. We got very paranoid and very unreasonable. After a couple of weeks, when Bravo squad rolled out the local shooting circus took a few hours off. We had slotted a good three dozen from various groups with extreme prejudice and they learned real fast that when it came to diplomacy, Bravo squad were no longer in a talking mood. It didn't hurt that after the first week, our roll outs sometimes had Ruza or Svila walking the rooftops on one side or the other.

Meanwhile, we struck up a working relationship with Delta squad. Charlie squad were all new, but Delta's core team had survived the hillside incident and had come back up to strength with three lads from Swift's old outfit. The combination was a winner as far as we were concerned, because it doubled our numbers for the piece of insanity we were working on.

Ruza and Svila gave us a lot of intel that the brass would have killed for, but we couldn't take a chance that Bad Raven had people ready to tip him off. So Kristof got some of the local 'good' government lads and lassies on our team.

Two months after Skinner and I staggered in from the wilderness, we were ready to give our pet hate a very bad night. We started it slow, just some official raids on outlying strongholds and safe houses. Then the government lads hit one of his biggest black market supply depots. Sure enough, the private security goons rolled out from a completely unflagged location which we got the heads up on from a very winded but smiling kid. When the government lads called for help, Sarge was ready to roll out Delta squad, loaded for bear and riding a Warrior that he had freed up by some obscure deal with the boys over in armour. The advantage with that, apart from bigger guns, was the recording gear on board. An hour later we had footage of the private security goons, recognised as official NATO forces, engaged in a firefight with friendly government forces and continuing even after those forces clearly identified themselves. Of course, at this point the filming stopped and the Warrior's firepower made short work of the goons. With that footage, the whole thing fell apart as Sarge raised several sorts of hell with the MP and NATO. There were officers being arrested and Captain Dell was levelled by a six foot eight MP gorilla when he tried to pull a sidearm. Police vehicles screamed through the night and it looked like we'd kicked off a fine bit of mayhem to keep Bad Raven busy.

Which was Bravo squad's cue to roll out in a Saxon recovery vehicle, heading for the place where the unlamented private security knobs had come from. As we turned the corner away from the base, Ruza and Svila leapt on top and crouched down.

The place was a high-walled town house. As we rolled up we could see it was burning. We'd done our work a little too well and Bad Raven had done a runner instead of coming to sort us out. Corp was cursing something fierce when Svila tapped on his helmet as Ruza smiled.

"No need for helicopter. Skies are ours."

I shall treasure the look on Corporal Teak's face, as Svila jumped straight up into the air and sprouted wings, for the rest of my life.

With Svila acting as spotter, we headed out of town into the hills. The ambush that Bad Raven left for us ended up going very badly for them, but it bogged us down. In the end, Corp turned to me and Skinner.

"Take the Saxon and drive straight through them. We can keep them from messing with you but you and the –"

He shook his head: "I still don't believe I'm saying this. You and the angels will have to bring him down."

The Saxon went through the roadblock with ease and we headed out after the *valravne*. About an hour later we had left the road far behind and as we turned off a dirt track onto some sort of cattle trail, an IED took out the back end of the Saxon. Sheer luck the front wheels had missed it. From there we walked, Ruza and Svila with their wings out and swords in hand. Ruza started talking as we yomped along the trail.

"He will be waiting along here somewhere, and we will have no warning. If I were him, I would use modern weapons before moving to powers. If he does, we will move the fight to somewhere between. It will be better for you."

Skinner chuckled.

"You mean that when he does whatever he's going to do, it'll probably kill us so our only chance is to fight him in the place where we're not dead."

I hated him sometimes.

Ruza laughed quietly and spoke rapidly to Svila, who patted Skinner's shoulder. As I looked back from that I saw a raised straight edge on the ground in front of me.

"Fu-"

The world exploded.

*

"Wake up you lazy bastard!"

Skinner's shout was more desperate than loud, and I opened my eyes to the evening twilight of somewhere else. We were surrounded by tall trees with narrow trunks and across the clearing something with smoke for wings and claws for hands was giving Svila a hard time. So I stood up, pulled my Browning and shot it in the head. Twice. It dropped like sack of spuds. Then I looked about.

Svila moved to lean against a tree, leaking dark claret from a wound in her side. Skinner was lying on my right, left arm missing and face slashed up so badly it looked like someone had ploughed it. Ruza? Where was Ruza? I was turning back to check Skinner when I saw ugly twitch a smoky wing.

With a loud curse I strode across the clearing to it, stomped my boot down on its throat and put the rest of my magazine into it's head. I was turning away when a tremor under my boot really pissed me off.

"Hell's teeth! Svila, your sword."

I held my hand out and she passed it to me. Without ceremony I rammed the blade right through the things chest and drove the tip a good few inches or so into the ground under it.

"Stay."

With that, I turned to look for Ruza again. There she was, coming through the trees at a run, wings up and sword low. She was magnificent. Never understood that word until then. I was just savouring the moment when something smashed my pelvis and most things around it by sheer brute force from behind. I lay there gasping as Ruza came past, my shrinking vision framing her against trees reduced to purple smudges as my blurring sight added a blue haze to her, wings mantling as she hurtled toward whatever had done for me. As she left my oval of sight, I saw her sword start to come forward in a low swing. Out of my sight, I heard a very solid thunk and the sound of wood splintering. An inhuman scream of fury and pain cut off as suddenly as it started. I was drifting on the edge of consciousness chuckling inside over how many times I had blacked out in Ruza's presence when I did it again.

*

I woke up with an angel kissing me and a feeling like someone was pushing blunt needles through my testicles. Ruza let go and I screamed for about a minute before collapsing in a heap. After a while I summoned the energy to roll my head sideways. Svila lay a little way from me, her head cradled in Skinner's lap. He was leaning against a tree. He looked like shit.

She looked like someone had shot her in the head a - oh, no! I looked up at Ruza. She laid her hand on my cheek.

"The *valravne* took her appearance and smothered her in illusion as we arrived. The explosion was very big and threw me a long way off. Svila will recover as you are not quite powerful enough to kill her. He was too arrogant to finish her as he thought he could trick you into doing it. But I have had to use all of my remedies on her. On you and Skinner, I could only use my choosing to let the both of you live. You will be in pain for a long time and you may not walk again, Jensen."

I smiled and croaked, "Breach of contract, call upstairs."

Ruza looked puzzled.

"How can I stand with the angels if I can't stand? And the angels must be able to stand for us to stand with them?"

Skinner's voice was hoarse but his tone was clear: "Svila says you're a crap shot."

Ruza barked laughter to the skies and suddenly stopped. She looked back at me, a look of wonder around the smile on her face.

"He agrees. But mentioned you must not be calling him 'upstairs' ever again."

I ran out of words. Then I screamed and arched from the ground as I experienced the unique sensations of my shattered pelvis reassembling itself under divine influence. Yet again, I passed out in Ruza's arms.

*

Something reached through the coma and wrote a memory for me: Of a winged woman delivering two broken men back to the remains of their squad. Of helicopters and emergency medical centres. Of looking out the porthole of a Hercules flying over water to see a redheaded angel carrying a blonde angel just behind us. Of operating theatres and doctors shaking their heads. Of a red-haired nurse who only came at night. Of a surgeon closing a clipboard and saying: "I have no idea. It's another one for the 'we don't talk about it' cabinet."

*

Eventually I woke up at my parent's place in Norfolk. Skinner was sitting next to my bed, reading a book held in a fancy artificial hand. He looked up as I turned my head.

"Hello, skinny git. You took a long time getting back."

I had been out of it for nearly a year. Invalided out of the army, decorated in absentia, full care. Skinner got a gong too and a medical discharge as he was down an arm.

I guess the powers upstairs had no problem fixing me, it was just an oversight or a pointed lesson that they did not turn the pain off as they did it. The pain was the problem: it sent me catatonic. After that, it was just time. Ruza and Svila stayed for while after Svila recovered, but as Skinner sensitively put it: "Bored women are a pain. Bored Valkyries who can't cook for shit are murder."

While I've been out of it, Skinner has been in touch with and spent some time with the folk back in Sarajevo. We're apparently up and running over there with Etherington Bailey as local liaison, plus some of the lads demobbed from Bravo and Delta squads, rounded out by Kristof and some of his now ex-government crew from that last confrontation. Romeo Sierra Security is who we are. A Sarajevo Rose is our logo. We never forget who pays the real price of war and we have angels on our fire team.

Give us a call if the bad guys are winning.

***

ANDE⊕: GL⊕SSARY

(Please note that any grammatical or technical misuse is wholly my fault.)

AK-47	Avtomat Kalashnikova 1947, the most widely-used assault rifle in the world
Andeo	Angel (Serbian)
Andeli u paklu	Angels in hell (Serbian)
APC	Armoured personnel carrier
Bikkja	Bitch (Old Norse)
Book	Retreat
Browning	Browning Hi-Power 9mm semi-automatic pistol, standard sidearm of the British Army
Claret	Blood
Clocked	Seen
CQC	Close Quarters Combat; a specialised group of fighting techniques
Demobbed	Demobilised. To leave the armed forces.
Gildr	Worthy (Old Norse)
Gong	Medal
HST	High-Speed Train
Hercules	Lockheed C-130K Hercules transport aircraft (designated as the Hercules C.1 by the RAF)
IED	Improvised Explosive Device
Kvedja	Greetings (Old Norse)
Landie	Land Rover
LSW	Light support weapon; the L86 variant of the SA80
Minimi	Light machine gun; the FN Minimi

MOD	Ministry of Defence
MP	Military Police
NATO	North Atlantic Treaty Organisation
PBI	Poor Bloody Infantry
Rabbited	Running as fast as possible
RE	Religious Education – a class in UK secondary schools
Recce	Reconnaissance
ROE	Rules Of Engagement
RPG	Rocket-propelled grenade
Ruza	Rose (Serbian)
SA80	UK rifle 'family'; variant L85A1 in this case
Sarajevo Rose	The impact pattern of a mortar shell on hard ground is unique and can resemble a flower. In Sarajevo, those that caused the death of innocents had that scar filled with red resin
Saxon	British armoured personnel Carrier. Variant AT105E
Slashers	Nickname for the Royal Gloucestershire Regiment
Slot	Kill
Solingen	Combat knife manufactured in Solingen, the 'City of Blades'
Stag	Watch
Strazar	Guardsman (Serbian)
Svila	Silk (Serbian)
Tabbing	Marching with full kit
Tama	Shadow (Serbian)
Valravne	Raven of the Slain (Danish)
Vardmadr	Watcher (Old Norse)
Vlasnik	Lord (Serbian)

Warrior	British FV-150 Warrior Infantry Fighting Vehicle
Yomp	Walking over mixed terrain with usual kit. Less implied urgency and load than 'tabbing'.

***

DRAGON QUEEN

A tale contemporary with The Hunter, but
set in the mythical lands to the East of Khyr.

The night was dark and cold with Wulf away. No matter that the high tower was brightly lit with candles and the furs were warm from lying in front of the blazing fire, some nights she just could not sleep without him.

The lair is warm and dry and the hatchlings are clamouring for a story.

She smiled. Jarath could always sense her moods. She picked up a worn notebook from one of the many dressers and made her way down to the great hall. Sliding behind the huge tapestry depicting the Fall of Tarantia, she opened the vaulted door using the words Jarath had taught her. Pausing only to ensure that the thick door swung silently closed behind her, she took the wide obsidian stairs down to the caves at the heart of the mountain. As she wound round the last long spiral, the cave opened to her view: a vast expanse of stalactites and stalagmites rising from a floor covered in the riches of nations. Jarath was a drake of restraint, but for his family he had made a liberal exception. Speaking of his family, she saw Allethare sleeping off to one side, her crimson hide shining with the hand-searing warmth of her pregnancy. Another clutch in the summer. She turned her attention to spotting the current clutch before they swooped on her.

They are here. I told them that antics were not a good way to persuade you to tell them a tale from our past.

She smiled and then laughed out loud. Gathered at the foot of the stairs were all four of Jarath and Allethare's hatchlings. Barely a year old, they were each already bigger than a merchant wagon. Their wings mantled as they saw her and their eager hisses blew a warm draught around her bare legs.

Manners!

Jarath was a stern father, but she appreciated it. It was difficult enough to make the locals understand that the dragons of Hellengard Peak had no interest in descending *en masse* and stealing their gold and virgins. The occasional hatchling sized piece of childish mayhem and ruination would have made it near impossible.

A fantastically striped hatchling bowed its head to the floor, then turned its head to look back at its sire, lost in the shadows.

𝔥ebeneth apologises for blowing your robes about and asks that you tell them all a story because it's a good night for it, apparently.

Ascorea, Dragon Queen of Hellengard, threw her head back and laughed. She could feel Jarath's restrained humour at his son's extreme politeness combined with his deep pride in his clutch.

"I would be delighted to tell such well behaved hatchlings a tale."

She cocked an imperious beckoning hand toward the deeper dark that showed where Jarath lay.

"But only if daddy gets his lazy bones over here for me to recline on."

The hatchlings went off in fits of draconic cackling as the shadowed form rose to its feet.

𝔩 spend months teaching them respect and this is how you reward me? Evil child, 𝔩 should have left you to Berd the 𝔉at.

Ascorea smiled as her oldest friend hove into view. Then she gasped.

"Jarath Demonburner, you have grown again!"

Jarath turned a head to regard his massive frame as he manoeuvred with uncanny agility and unerring step to lay down in a suitably silver coated field of treasure.

It seems that the results of multiple successful clutches are beneficial for all participants. I am now the biggest drake outside of Khyr.

Ascorea skipped across the floor to stretch herself in the monstrous chaise-longue formed as he tucked his forearm against the side of his chest. She looked up the wall of purple scales to his head high above.

"There's a dragon bigger than you in Khyr? Ye gods."

Bane.

She saw the hatchlings shiver at the mention of that nemesis' name. She moved to dispel the mood from that.

"Ah. Then I shall consider you the biggest dragon in the known world and have done. Now, you four. As your father mentioned Berd the Fat, would you like to hear how Jarath rescued me from being a scullion for my whole life?"

Gem like eyes whirled and glittered as the four settled themselves. Suddenly a humming started in Jarath's throat. It was like a cat's purr, yet carried such overt power and a feeling of intense safety.

You better not fluff this, dear child. Allethare is awake. She has been curious for years about our meeting.

Ascorea looked up to see a monstrous crimson and gold head settle on a pile of bejewelled armour to the far side of the spiral stairway. Time to put Jarath's years of painstaking teaching in draconic etiquette to good use.

"Greetings, Hestyr Allethare."

AND TO YOU, WAR QUEEN.

Ascorea nearly fell from her perch in surprise. Allethare's mindspeech was precise but the incredible echoing of the words in her head was stunning. She looked up at Jarath.

"Thanks for the warning."

Nothing to do with me. She said that, as she and you shared me, it was only fair that the womenfolk who rule my life could conspire against me without me acting as a translator.

Ascorea giggled. Now that was something she never considered. She turned to Allethare again and slapped Jarath's flank as she spoke.

"After you have clutched, we should have a chat about this monster in our midst."

i would like that. By then i should be able to mindspeak without rendering your wits unto jelly.

That would be good, thought Ascorea, wincing as the echoes in her head slowly faded.

Monster? Evil child, I can always take you back to Berd the Fat, you know. Now do tell the story before the little monsters get restless.

She smiled. So long ago. She opened her first notebook and looked at the four hatchlings in front of her.

"I first met your father when I was only nine and he was only huge."

Do behave. A little decorum, please.

She grinned as she scanned the childish block capitals in the notebook, then closed it, looked up and closed her eyes. She only needed to read the first sentence to recall the whole series of events that changed her life forever.

*

"Dear diary. Today a dragon landed on the barn. Daddy was really angry after he finished hiding."

Angry wasn't quite the right word, but Suzanna didn't know the correct one to put in her notebook so it would have to do. She listened to Daddy rant and shout downstairs while Brother Gabbett tried to calm him and stop him blaspheming.

"What am I supposed to do, Gabbett? Always said that bloody dragons were going to ruin us and with one landing on the barn I cannot make my tithe to Lord Traffen's seneschal tomorrow. Where's this divine protection you keep banging on about? I tithe better than any around here yet I have a dragon in my barn!"

With the last few words, Suzanna's father's voice cracked and he sat in a fit of coughing. She moved slowly so the boards wouldn't creak. She wanted to hear what Brother Gabbett had to say.

"On the morrow, good Thomas, I shall go forth with the Book of Teth in hand and accompanied by a spirit of innocence. With that, Blessed Teth will cause the beast to flee."

"Spirit of innocence? What's that?"

"Your youngest, good man. It is written that these creatures cannot stand against the twin forces of the holy word and the eyes of an innocent."

Suzanna hugged herself. She was going to meet the dragon! How wonderful would that be? She listened to her Daddy rant hoarsely for a bit longer but it did seem that his resistance was weakened by the thought of being able to salvage the fruits of his harvest.

The next morning, just after dawn, Brother Gabbett collected Suzanna from her mother as soon as she was washed and dressed. He sprinkled her with holy water and pronounced her best dress to be ideal for her part. With no further ceremony he grabbed her hand and marched out of the kitchen, his other hand clutching his aged and battered Book of Teth. Brandishing it high in the air, he stormed across the yard toward the ruins of the barn, where gaps in the riven planking revealed purple scales shining in the early sunlight. Brother Gabbett was chanting litany in a surprisingly clear tenor, the sweat of fervour and fear mingling on his brow. Suzanna was disappointed that she could not understand the priest. It must be good if it could make a dragon go away.

Oh for pity's sake, a priest of Teth dragging a child to scare me off. Can't a legendary predator get a day's sleep in peace?

Suzanna stood completely still. That voice hadn't been in her ears, it had been in her head! Brother Gabbett broke his chant to look down at her with a kindly smile.

"Don't be frightened child. It cannot harm you while you're under Teth's protection."

Don't be so stupid, priest; the child is safe because I would lose my wings before harming a hatchling of any breed.

Suzanna couldn't help it. She giggled. Brother Gabbett muttered under his breath

"Dear Teth, don't let the girl go mad. The damned creature will eat me for sure."

Maybe it would be good for the clergy if I ate the priest? No, they would only say he was impure as the child was left alive. Blessed Sun but I hate self-insulating religions.

Suzanna was curious.

"Brother Gabbett, what is a self-insulating religion?"

The good brother stopped dead in his tracks, chant forgotten in surprise. He looked at her as a crash echoed from the barn.

"Who told you those words, child? They are mordant blasphemy."

If you can hear me child, tell the priest that you heard a peddler muttering them last week as he left the farm after he traded with your father.

Suzanna did as suggested. Brother Gabbett looked relieved.

"Very good, child. I shall mention this to the Holy Father tonight and we might be able to get the blasphemer restrained."

I doubt it. That peddler was my brother in shape-changed form and he's two hundred miles away eating a fat merchant right now.

Suzanna giggled again. This seemed to remind Brother Gabbett of his more immediate concerns. Brandishing the book high, he positively stormed toward the barn, his chant at double speed and Suzanna running to keep up.

Child, I am going to have to leave before the fool priest forces me to do something rude so I can have some peace. If you would like to continue this chat, just say which window in the farmhouse is yours.

Suzanna smiled. She had been talking to a dragon and he was offering to come back and talk properly! She whispered a reply.

"Other side, second in the roof from this end."

Good girl. See you just after moonset tomorrow morning.

With that, the barn exploded as a huge purple dragon took off from within it and glided westward toward the wild lands. Brother Gabbett was in raptures.

"You see! Teth's grace is incontestable by creatures of evil! All praise to him!"

Idiot.

Suzanna had to feign a coughing fit to cover the giggles that the scathing observation from far away caused.

With the dragon gone, the rest of the day was spent clearing up the mess, after the best of the salvaged foodstuffs was carefully placed in tithing bags ready for Lord Traffen's seneschal to arrive. He finally appeared in the early afternoon, cut off Thomas' explanation with a brusque: "Protection from dragons is work for Teth's faithful." and departed as soon as his men had loaded the tithe without even accepting a stirrup cup.

Suzanna was in a daze of anticipation and dread all day. Everyone put it down to her near death at the fangs and claws of a savage dragon. So when she asked if she could go to bed early, the request was granted and her mother brought her some hot, spiced milk a little later.

She lay there trembling. What if the dragon didn't come back? What if he was only coming back to get a snack? What if he was coming back because it was wrong for little girls to hear dragons? She was just starting to create even wilder reasons for the dragon not coming at all or only coming to eat her when she fell asleep.

Good morning.

Suzanna was awake instantly. A huge head blocked the view through the window, but the light of the crimson eyes turned her little room into a magical grotto. She sat up in bed, head swivelling frantically as she tried to take it all in.

Slow down, child. There is time enough. No—one in your house will wake before dawn. Make your way downstairs and we can talk out in the yard.

Suzanna did so. The house was eerie and even the dogs lay in front of the hearth oblivious to the talkative monster outside. She stepped out and found she did not need the shawl she had brought. The dragon radiated a comfortable heat. She stood and leaned back as her gaze travelled up him to his head.

"You're really big."

I am Jarath and I am delighted to meet a dragonspeaker.

"Is that what I am?"

Indeed it is. You are the first to be found before the church claimed your soul in a very long time.

"That doesn't sound good."

It means that the church will kill you and probably your family too because they are scared of people who can speak to dragons.

"But if I don't tell them?"

Very good. The other dragonspeakers were slain because they thought the church would be interested in speaking with us, so they went to the clergy. Thankfully we met yesterday and with a little help, I think you and I could have a lot of fun.

"Fun?"

You keep this a secret and I will visit occasionally. When you've grown enough I will be able to take you flying. If you like it, when you come of age, you can come away with me.

"How long will that be?"

I think you'll be big enough to ride on me in two years or so. You will need to exercise a lot between now and then. After that, we will have to wait until you are seventeen. If your ability to talk to me does not fade at the solstices before your eighteenth birthday, then you are a true dragonspeaker and I would welcome a chance to travel with you.

Suzanna though long and hard for a nine year old. After a couple of minutes, she had reached a decision.

"Thank you, Jarath. I think I would like that but I would like to wait and see. My mummy says not to make big choices fast."

Your mother is very wise. Now I can hear a patrol coming, so you had better go back to bed and don't forget your shawl. I will return at the dark of the moon every second month. Let us see how we get on.

*

With that, Suzanna's life changed. She had a gift like no other and a secret beyond belief. At the dark of every second moon, Jarath would come to see her. She followed his instructions and her parents were delighted that the encounter with faith and a monster had transformed their daughter from a slothful fourth child into a hard working credit to the family. She also showed a remarkable interest and talent for numbers and letters, much to Brother Gabbett's delight. By her eleventh birthday, Suzanna had had a growth spurt and was showing early signs of the beauty she would become. But she did not care. On the second dark of the moon after her eleventh birthday, she was waiting with baited breath for Jarath to come and take her flying.

ℌello Suzanna.

She jumped. How could something that big be so quiet?

"Hello Jarath. Am I big enough to fly with you tonight?"

You are. Let us see if you and the heavens like each other.

With that, Jarath crouched down and extended his right claw. Suzanna scrambled up onto his back and found a beautifully worked saddle on his back, ahead of his wings.

"Oh, this is lovely. Where did you get it?"

ℌer name was Ashelaine and she led the dragons of these lands to war three centuries ago. We have kept everything of hers in the hope that we would find another war queen one day.

"So I lead you for fighting?"

You do. Or you could if you decide to come away. Also, although you are titled war queen, you would have times of peace as well.

"Why do I lead you to war? I'm tiny."

It's not just you. There is something about having a dragonspeaker able to speak our magicks that makes the war queen and her chosen into something that very little can stand against.

"You would have to be my chosen, Jarath. I don't know any other dragons."

Jarath looked back at her as she figured out the straps on the saddle.

That was my hope. Shall we save further discussion of possible futures until we have determined that you can deal with the now?

Suzanna laughed at his tone.

"Good idea. Is there a magic word I need to say?"

No. But if you need to shout or scream there is nothing to stop you. Do what you feel. Ready?

Suzanna braced herself, a mad smile on her face.

"Go."

With a colossal lurch, Jarath ascended so fast that Suzanna forgot to breathe. Then he levelled off into a glide and circled the farm. Suzanna was entranced. No, more than that. She was home. Jarath looked back at her.

Had enough?

She laughed, tears in her eyes.

"Never. Fly me to the stars, Jarath."

One day when your powers can keep you alive out there. Until then, let us have some of that fun I promised you.

Jarath flapped his wings and they shot forward and slipped into a climb, Suzanna wound her neck about to try and see everything. Jarath kept climbing until they were looking down on the clouds. He glided again and looked back at her,

Now we shall see what you will be, little one.

He suddenly furled his wings and dropped toward the clouds. Suzanna screamed in terror and delight. Just as they were about to hit the cloud, she felt Jarath vibrate underneath her and he shot a huge gout of flame from his mouth, vapourising the clouds ahead so they hurtled through a hot, misty tunnel illuminated by his fiery breath. As they shot out of the base of the cloud, Jarath rolled over and ascended into the grey again. Suzanna's stomach was in her neck and then her bottom and for a moment she felt like she weighed more than an ox. Then they burst through the high cloud and the cool air chilled the moisture on her skin as the stars shone so bright, so close. Suzanna stared. Then she let out a shriek of pure joy. She screamed, she laughed, she sang snatches of her favourite songs. Running out of words, she wriggled in excitement and bounced up and down in the saddle. Jarath took them up again and then glided a while as he turned to look her over.

I get the feeling that you are utterly at home up here, aren't you?

Suzanna took a moment to rediscover a vocabulary.

"I love it. Love it. Never take this away. This moment. It's perfect."

Nearly. Wait until we do this under a full moon. Then hold that memory until we do it all under the summer sun.

"How long?"

Six years and eleven moons, Suzanna. Until then, we can only fly occasionally as it is a great risk to you and your family. But I promise that you will fly on the dark of the moon after your birthdays without fail. Enough future, let us have some more scream—worthy fun until I have to take you home.

The next day, Suzanna was so depressed. Walking seemed to be so tawdry in comparison to flying on a dragon. But she remembered Jarath's rules. She had to exercise as much as possible. She had to improve her reading, writing and arithmetic. She needed to learn as many languages as she could get from Brother Gabbett.

*

That was how it continued until her fourteenth birthday. By then, her father had got used to dismissing potential suitors from the surrounding farms. But two years of bad crops had taken its toll on his resolve. He was three daughters down and deep in debt. So when Berd the Fat, son of the seneschal, started to make overtures regarding his comely fourth daughter, he regarded it as providence from Teth. He was less than pleased at Suzanna's reaction. Indeed, he thought the white-faced shock, hysteria and running away was quite excessive. He cautioned her sternly and informed her that she would marry her chosen suitor.

Three days later, Jarath took the news with a calm that eased her worry.

This was always a possibility. I have a solution, but I doubt you will like it.

"Does it keep me out of the same bed as a naked Berd the Fat?"

Totally.

"Then I love it. What am I doing?"

You will confess to Brother Gabbett that the thought of marriage feels wrong to you.

"Absolute truth. My husband-to-be weighs more than some of the cattle he eats.

You feel that Teth may have a purpose for you, for why else would you be interested in such unwomanly pursuits as learning languages and studying?

"All good so far."

Then you request that Brother Gabbett cloister you immediately to prevent your father or indeed the seneschal interfering. After that, it should be simple to have yourself taken to Ambesford Cloisters. You will only be able to cloister yourself for four years, but in that time you can expand your learning considerably.

"Brilliant!"

Suzanna fell silent as a bad thought intruded.

"I won't be able to see you at all, will I?"

Jarath rested his head on the ground next to her.

That is the problem. I will come if you call me, but apart from that I will not see you until your eighteenth birthday as you are returned to the world from the cloisters.

Suzanna laid herself along his long snout and hugged him.

"I will miss you but it is the only way without me becoming a scullion for the seneschal's son."

You will have one other task to divert you in the cloisters.

"That would be?"

Finding yourself a name. As our war queen, you cannot let your true name be known. So you must choose one that will become your name to the world.

Suzanna liked that idea a lot. A new name for a new life. She bade a sad farewell to Jarath and went to get some sleep. The following day was going to be difficult.

It was more than difficult, it was almost impossible. She actually had to flee from her own father to make it to Brother Gabbett's tiny shrine to Teth. She confessed all and Brother Gabbett, convinced that her witnessing his turning of the dragon all those years ago had predisposed her to serving Teth for the rest of her life, was only too happy to shrive and cloister her immediately. She nearly fumbled her vows as Jarath interjected from far away:

I revise my opinion of him from idiot to fool misguided by idiots.

*

Suzanna entered Ambesford Cloisters to the frustration of her father and Berd the Fat, although her mother sympathised but dared say nothing. On her sixteenth birthday, her mother informed her that she would emerge from cloisters directly into marriage. The arrangement had been sanctioned by the recently endowed Baron Traffen and dowry had been given. The fact that the timing of the dowry payment kept the family farm out of the clutches of the money lenders and producing for Traffen was quietly overlooked. Her mother told her father that Suzanna had taken the news remarkably well. He thanked Teth for guiding his daughter into acceptance of the life chosen for her at last.

Within the cloisters, Suzanna had gained a reputation as hardworking and studious. She showed her devotion in the practical arts and in the transcription of old texts, producing safe versions of old works for use by the faithful.

The only idiosyncrasy she had was that she liked to spend the entire night before her birthday in a vigil on the watchtower. This was tolerated as she showed none of the flightiness or daydreaming tendencies of the other girls. If this was her only eccentricity, it was one that could be accepted.

The day before her eighteenth birthday, she impressed the sisters by donating all of her possessions to her companions. The snide commented that her marriage would provide her with everything she needed. She did not seem to mind. That night as she ascended the watchtower steps, it was remarked upon how serene she looked.

*

It was a beautiful clear night with just the faintest sliver of a new moon. Suzanna knelt in her usual place by the crenellated outer wall of the observation post until the sisters departed. As the night settled to silence about her, she waited. This was it. The final hours of nine years of waiting. With a smile, she unbound her hair and stood to let her robes fall. Stepping from them, she stood silent and naked before the stars and made some vows that the sisters would not have approved of. She was just beginning to feel the cold when the sound of great wings sounded high above.

Happy birthday, war queen. How shall we call you?

Suzanna looked up as Jarath glided softly down. She climbed up on the battlement and prepared to jump. She looked back at the cloisters and then looked east toward her parent's farm. With a smile and tentative wave, she bid Suzanna goodbye.

"Ascorea."

Ah, the mythical star that the pilgrim hopes to see to tell him that his journey is done. Are you done with your former life, child?

She had no doubts anymore.

"I am."

She heard wings in the dark and saw a dozen great drakes sweep low behind Jarath.

My kindred, Ascorea of the East March steps freely into the saddle and mantle of Ashelaine. We have a war queen once more.

Ascorea jumped from the battlement without a qualm, her trust in her chosen total. She landed on his back, seated herself quickly and strapped herself in. She took a deep breath.

"Let's fly, my Jarath. I've been waiting so long to come home."

Indeed, my Ascorea. Let us fly.

And they were gone.

*

Suzanna of Tilbride farm ascended to Teth on the morn of her eighteenth birthday. She was sanctified a week later on the testimony of one Brother Gabbett, who swore that her presence had driven forth a great dragon from her father's barn. She had only been nine years of age at the time. Her parents recounted how that experience had turned her from a lazy girl into a model daughter. The sisters testified as to her diligence and her generosity on the eve of her ascension. All present testified to her calm acceptance of the hostility of others and her look of transcendent calm upon walking up to the roof of the watchtower that final time. The clothing she had shed at the moment of her divine embrace was duly transferred to a sanctified ark that resides to this day on the very spot of her ascension. Brother Gabbett received special dispensation to remain at the cloisters to tend her shrine. Her holy presence is regarded as sovereign protection from any evil creature, especially dragons.

*

Idiots.

"Jarath. Behave."

***

THE LAST DRUID

A tale of one possible future for the world of 'These Pagan Isles'. One that I sincerely hope will never come to pass.

The autumn leaves were sere and wasted: great drifts of gold and brown crumbling steadily to dust as far as he could see. The trunks of the ancient trees were dark in the shade of the setting sun, yet softly lit like relief maps on their sunward sides with creeping shadows filling the rugose textures of the bark like valleys seen from high above. He squashed his last cigarette betweens his calloused fingers and pushed himself up against the great yew that dominated this part of the valley. Taking a careful breath, he began:

"Spirit of the land, take this world,"
"With all its autumnal colours furled."

His voice wasn't what it used to be, years of smoking and trekking between settlements in the empty vastnesses, living off the slim pickings, all the while breathing the nacreously-veined air had taken its toll. He smiled. Ruby had always said that smoking would be the death of his bardic voice and to deny the world that would be a crime. She hadn't said anything about the world taking the bard and leaving him smoking. He continued:

"Spirit of this place, take me whole,"
"Weave me back into the earth's great soul."

Around him, fire sprites clattered, waiting for his permission. Their little eyes spun and shed light like pairs of fireflies in formation. Not long now, Brighid's children, he thought. They were as nature itself, beautiful and deadly to the weak, the evolutionary failures. He smiled. Darwin would have nodded his head in agreement had he seen what man had done to fail so spectacularly. He nodded in time to a tune unheard for decades as he felt the third stanza rise:

"Spirit of this elder tree, take my words,"
"Weep for the songs never to be heard."

Songs unheard. So very true. As any dead organic matter crumbled swiftly to dust unless of a substantial size, instruments were gone - apart from the abominations created from bone or plastic, but they did not sound the same and had spirits of cold mien. How ironic that centuries of learning had gone in days, yet the bags and binders used to protect them had survived. The fourth stanza came suddenly:

"Spirit of the sky, look down with sorrow,"
"At a race denied atonement tomorrow."

Not surprising, really. Man had abused his position so badly for centuries, the fireplagues and dustdeath were an obvious culmination of a war fought so subtly no-one noticed until too late. Nature had always evolved ways to balance itself, but as man rose to dizzying technological heights, his ability to cure or contain any new blight or perceived threat outstripped Nature's ability to produce balancing agents. With wondrous advances in medical science, fertility increased, infant death became negligible and life spans exceeded two centuries. So Nature moved to work in the new home of evolution, the laboratories of man. The fifth stanza came easily:

"Spirit of the waters so long unseen,"
"Rise again to make fields of green."

The breakdown of the weather systems as pollution accelerated the gradual rhythm of an approaching ice age was unexpected, but man responded by establishing weather control at last. Who needed currents and evaporation, they said, when we can make it happen to order? That had been fine until the great solar flare flash-fried all of the delicate quantum tech and nano-electronics so essential to the overcrowded utopia that Earth had become. A global infrastructure failure took only a day and completely overwhelmed every remediation plan. Break a little, there were parts. Break it all and wars were fought over the remaining parts. Pyrrhic victory was defined in those clashes as frequently the parts were destroyed in the wars raged over their possession. Stanza six ripped through his memories:

"Spirit of the air, this glowing death,"
"Purge the poisons from your toxic breath."

The visible air syndrome had just happened. The stuff you were so used to breathing unseen became visible. It glowed. The warmer the environment, the brighter it was. Rumours pointed to a couple of governments desperately releasing an airborne agent to combat the fireplagues. It seemed logical to him. Especially as it slew all domesticated livestock within a few months. Most larger mammals went too in a year or so. Man had a couple of decades of mutations, frantic genetic engineering and accusations before the insidious poison rendered humanity sterile. The eighth stanza came like a balm to his parched throat:

"Lady bless the world we leave,"
"Lord make better heirs to receive."

Of course, the global catastrophes were religion's gain. Suddenly a huge percentage of mankind rediscovered their god. Cults spread like wildfire as every fanatic with an even vaguely save-the-faithful agenda acquired a devoted following overnight. It was strangely fitting that in a time when every man should have been making peace with his gods, he was actually committing hideous atrocities in their name upon those who did not follow his particular flavour of salvation. Stanza nine crackled in his throat:

"Gods that pass and gods that wait,"
"Forgive the fools who awoke too late."

He smiled again as an owl hooted nearby. Some creatures just seemed to adapt to the new world like they had been waiting for it. Polar bears, owls and wolves now preyed on a huge diversity of reptiles. All of them preyed on man. Man who huddled in enclosed enclaves with treadmill powered air purifiers running night and day, collecting every last drop of dew and recycling their waste as food until it became only barely useful as mulch for their stunted crops. When he had been called to the long road, communities were roughly a day apart and bandit gangs roamed free. After the first decade, the settlements were a few days apart and bandits were non-existent. Year on year, he would find settlements abandoned and a longer walk to the next one. Five years ago he had failed to find any inhabited settlements. Since then, he had walked, chanted, hoped and prayed his way across three continents. A month ago he had felt the burning in his gut and turned for home. Or what had been home, a century and a half before. Two weeks ago he had struggled across the plastic islands of the toxic swamp that had been the English Channel. Three days ago he had crested the rise and walked down into Kingley Vale. He had walked the vale slowly until this great tree had revealed itself, and he knew his time was come. He had finished his meagre provisions, drunk a final, precious dram of mead with the moon last night and finished his last smoke a few minutes ago. Now the sun was nearly gone, only the tops of the trees showing light.

He hoped whatever came next treated this world a damn sight better than his kindred had. Stanza ten seemed to elude him as his breath shortened and the burning spread through his chest. Just as he was about to panic over not finishing, he realised even the stanzas were done. With a smile, he breathed his last:

"Awen."

***

FIRE IN MIND

A tale from the today of 'These Pagan Isles' - a world not quite as mundane as some would have us believe.

I could not remember my name as the flames shaped themselves into warriors of amber and gold. I watched as the blazing soldiers stormed the keep on the hill, orange shields held close to their bodies, swords of yellow streaked with red raised and heedless of the fiery moat that seemed to be inescapable. But their cinder-soled boots allowed them to rush straight across the obstacle and lay siege to the umber keep. The horde settled in a ring of little flames on the blackened hill, the ground riven with cracks showing the red-hot earth below. What rage could have started this? What fury?

"Marty?"

"Martin!"

My vision collapsed into whirling points of light and I felt my mind recoil as the flames seemed to rush into my eyes. I blinked, my eyes sore and dry. Looking about, I saw Katy standing by me, a look of annoyed concern on her face. She proffered a bottle of water before crouching down.

"Off watching movies in the fire again, eh?"

I growled and mumbled as I bathed my eyes and face before taking a long swig from the bottle. My vision had been reduced to black and white, but it was night so it didn't matter. I smiled at Katy.

"Yeah, it was a good one too. Right up there with 'Slaughtermaster'."

Katy rolled her eyes and slapped me on the back of the head.

"You're impossible. Get your arse in gear, stew's on and Mike's hungry, so be bloody quick."

I stared back at the fire, but Katy was ready and pinched my earlobe. Suitably chastened, I straightened up slowly, stretching high and wide. I must have been crouched by the fire for a good half hour. I looked again and stumbled as my strained vision caught a pair of eyes regarding me from the flames. I stopped to gain my balance, rubbed my eyes and looked back at the fire. The eyes remained. Very slowly, the right one closed and opened. I decided that I had done way to much fire-gazing on an empty stomach. Time to eat and then write up that siege before we gathered around the fire again for the evening's entertainment.

The evening passed rapidly, the songs getting sillier and more ribald as the alcohol took effect. The stories lapsed to anecdotes and then to jokes. Finally, the jokes turned old or bad or both, and people drifted away to their tents and caravans to either collapse or open another bottle. Either way, despite clear skies and a blazing fire, by midnight there was only Mike, Katy and I. They sat with me chatting desultorily for a half hour or so before adjourning to their tent. Katy stopped as they gathered their things and stared hard at me. She moved two bottles of water next to me.

"Don't spend too much time staring at the fire, you have to drive tomorrow."

I smiled at her. Sometimes she just could not keep the big sister part of her down.

"No probs, sis. I'll be good."

She shook her head, Mike slapped my shoulder and they were gone. The night slowed and quietened, the only rhythm the snapping of the fire. I added a few logs, pulled up a low chair and settled myself. There was no way I was going to waste this much time where I had the site and the fire to myself.

So there I sat, staring at the flames as my mind wrought pictures from the shapes. My writing gift had been spasmodic and useless until I discovered my fire-gazing. It had suddenly started during the second of these pagan camps I had been dragged to, about three years ago. Now I had a publishing deal after only one book, and early drafts of the sequel combined with the first were already being touted to film studios. This was of course the make or break moment. Either the book to come exceeded the surprise sales of the first and I went on to be an established writer with my novels adapted for film, or I joined the long list of also-rans, the one-book wonders.

Suddenly my vision did the strange loss of focus I was waiting for and I was staring at the aftermath of the siege, the umber keep blazing and the hordes spinning a mad victory dance around it as the defenders perished in the place they sought to save. I waited for the next chapter to reveal itself and while doing so became aware of movement around the base of the hill. A great scaled creature with furled wings and mighty claws stalked the dancing horde. I was waiting with baited breath for its attack when it suddenly sat back on its haunches, shook its wings and opened its mouth wide in a mighty yawn. Closing its mouth, it turned and looked straight at me with eyes familiar from earlier.

"You bored with churning out gutter pulp?"

I blinked, but while the umber keep and its conquerors vanished, the creature did not.

"Hello? I'm talking to the man with the look of disbelieving shock on his face."

I stammered something incomprehensible.

"English, man, English. Good grief, no wonder you're such a hack."

That did it. I hated being termed a hack writer. Admittedly I'd done my time in the local papers, but I was never a hack.

"How the hell would you know?"

"Because I am a child of Brighid and writers are my speciality. Plus you are keyed to fire."

"Whoa there. Brighid? As in Celtic goddess of fire and poetry?"

"An aspect of the maiden goddess and attributed to the Celts, yes. Fire, poetry, written arts, inspiration and the whole shebang in that neck of the woods."

I shook my head hard and pinched the bridge of my nose with eyes screwed tight shut. I opened them on hearing a low popping sound. The creature was clearly a miniature dragon in fiery hues as it stood next to the fire, setting the grass around itself to smouldering. It continued.

"Now, the acid test."

"What?"

It stalked forward.

"Either you go insane - catatonia or raving; I'm not sure which you'll be. Or you run away screaming."

I sat and regarded this apparition that curiously held no strangeness for me.

"Is there another option?"

It paused in its approach and regarded me.

"Yes. You let me ride with you."

"What?"

"You open yourself and accept me. Then you'll have fire inside, be able to write better and more. She likes that idea. Thought you had potential and thought I'd been idling around the halls a little too long."

"Halls?"

The dragon sat down hard, rolling its eyes.

"Always the questions. Halls, as in High Halls. Dwelling places of the gods and those that can get there if they can and are allowed."

I smiled.

"So you've been kicked out because you've been lazing around the home of the gods without doing any good stuff to deserve a place?"

The creature narrowed its eyes. Its voice was icy.

"You could interpret it like that."

"So as a punishment you get a task to make you pay for your sloth?"

The dragon settled down and laid its wings flat.

"You think it's funny only having a sense of self when you're between the humans you're meant to help? Once I'm in, I'm you. There's no little voice in your head... unless you have them already."

He cocked an eyebrow in query. I shook my head.

"No, no. All quiet in here."

With a fire spewing sigh, it stood up again.

"Decision time. Be a hack for the rest of your natural or give me a soul to blend with so you can be the writer you so desperately want to be."

I thought hard. Then my ingrained cynicism kicked in.

"This seems too good to be true. I get you in my head and suddenly I get to be a Shakespeare? Where's the catch?"

The creature stopped dead in its tracks. The look on its face was disappointment.

"There is no catch. This is a gift. Every now and then the powers see something good that could do greater good except for some limitations. So they extend a boon, something to help."

I wasn't buying that for one moment. No way. There was some hidden purpose.

"I don't believe you."

The creature actually shrunk before my eyes.

"I presume you won't be accepting the gift?"

"No. It just cannot be that simple."

The creature turned toward the fire.

"It is that simple, yet for some it is complicated. You need to give the Lady your trust."

I shook my head. I had sat through three days of this pagan stuff so I could sit by the fire and get visions that turned to cash when I wrote them up. The rest of it had passed me by.

"Thanks, but no thanks. I'm good as I am."

The dragon shrunk again then paused as a figure stepped into my peripheral vision from the left. A hand reached out to the little dragon, a cigarette smoking between the primary fingers. A deep but wondering voice followed it.

"Oh my Lady, one of your own. Take my thanks to her, little friend."

The creature actually doubled in size before wrapping its tail around the extended hand and rubbing its brow on the knuckles, then it snapped up the cigarette and leapt into the fire which swelled with a muted roar. I sat there and looked up at the gent standing next to me. He was busy rolling another cigarette and staring at the fire, whispering words under his breath. Completing the cigarette, he stepped forward and dropped it into the fire. Then he stepped back, started rolling another cigarette and turned to me.

"You're the bloke who wrote 'Slaughtermaster', aren't you?"

I smiled.

"Yes. What did you think of it?"

"Pretty classic sword and sorcery fare, just with the gore and sex cranked up to the maximum you can get away with these days. Rumour has it you've got a sequel in the works."

"I have. Got film interest too."

He nodded.

"I wish you the best. I haven't had a book published yet."

I nodded back. Then I had to ask.

"So what was the deal with the little dragon?"

"That little fellow was straight from the fire courts. I am impressed you declined whatever he offered."

"Why?"

"Because the writing gift comes from Her. Not how to write, but being a writer. The ability to see something and create a poem as a photograph of it that includes the emotion of the moment. The ability to write prose that moves people to tears. Both are precious gifts from Her."

I started to get a sinking feeling.

"How do you know I don't have it?"

He paused as he lit his cigarette. His eyes glittered in the lighter's flame.

"Because you're a writer, yet you have sat uncaring for three days as a huge gamut of life, wonder and magic swirled around you. You only want to stare into the fire. You don't want to feel every moment for the flame of inspiration."

I stared at him, frankly uncomprehending. He smiled.

"Let me see if this helps. When you write, do you get a surge, fragments of ideas and other stories popping up in the fever of creation?"

I shook my head. I saw pictures in the fire and went away to write them down. That was it. In the firelight, his smiled thinned and disappeared.

"At the risk of having a moment where if I explain you can never understand; what I have described is the gift you were offered tonight."

I felt a sweat start on my brow. He continued.

"I was lucky enough to have been born with it, or it arrived earlier than I can recall. I do know that turning it down is incomprehensible to me. The magic and inspiration that every day holds through sight enhanced with this is beyond belief."

I knew that tone, the fanatic edge. My expression must have betrayed my thoughts, because he stepped away from me, pausing only to look back once.

"I call it the 'fire in mind'. I give thanks for it every day and trust me when I say you have spurned a gift beyond value. Fare you well."

With that he was gone into the night beyond the firelight. A while later I saw one of the old four wheel drive trucks start up and rumble on out of the field from the direction he had ambled off to.

I stared at that fire all night, kept it well-stoked. I saw nothing.

Just before dawn, I saw what looked like a burning reel of film in the heart of the fire. That was the last thing I ever saw in a fire. These days I use whiskey and write for the local paper. It pays. Never liked sword and sorcery anyway.

***